Praise for *The Deep Green Sea*

"In *The Deep Green Sea* the weight of destiny has a nearly physical pull . . . Butler's effort to merge myth and history is a significant one, an attempt to frame a literature that has to do with more than telling stories, but speaks to the deepest core of who we are."
—David L. Ulin, *Salon*

"Slim, erotic and fable-like. . . . It's a book that picks up on many of Butler's abiding themes—the legacy of the Vietnam War, the clash of Vietnam's folklore and mysticism with American manners, the sexual currents that flow between Vietnamese women (often prostitutes) and American soldiers and veterans. . . . Butler is often, and deservedly, praised for his ability to climb inside the hearts and minds of his Vietnamese characters . . . Throughout the novel, Butler writes the kind of long, rhythmic, adjective-free sentences that are the sign of a writer working to cast a spell . . . His spare descriptions can be enormously evocative."
—Dwight Garner, *New York Times Book Review*

"Like the classical genre to which it aspires, *The Deep Green Sea* raises such fundamental moral questions as: What is the price of knowledge and of truth, and what is the difference between them? Do we commit a sin against others when we deceive ourselves? What happens when we try to protect those we love by lying to them? What is the price of memory, and what happens to those who attempt to extinguish it?"
—Susie Linfield, *Los Angeles Times*

"Butler deftly exploits the traits of a blossoming relationship to develop more sinister themes . . . [*The Deep Green Sea* is] beautifully put together and uses sex and love to poignant effect to show the consequences of war in ordinary lives."
—*Literary Review*

"Butler has visited Vietnam many times in his fiction, eschewing blood and guts in favor of examining the hearts and minds of those affected by wartime . . . What is amazing, though, is how delicately the author treads on this sensitive material, which in the wrong hands could easily have turned preposterous or laughable. The two principals alternately recount their affair, only slowly becoming aware of the imminent tragedy, which adds to the quiet poignancy of the tale . . . [An] eloquent novel."

—*Library Journal*

"[Butler] explores further into the territory he knows best, with a poetic treatment of the love between a modern Vietnamese woman, orphaned in the fall of Saigon in 1975, and a blue-collar Vietnam vet delving into his traumatic past . . . A sincere treatment of the ancient theme of love mixed up with war."

—*The Scotsman*

"*The Deep Green Sea* is remarkable in many ways, not least for its daring. . . . [It] flirts with contradictions. It seems to be realistic but it turns out, it's not. It's a large adult fairy tale. It is also a short book, but not a quick read. The story moves at two speeds at once, much as 'Oedipus Rex' does, giving the impression that time is speeding by and is standing almost still. The reader wants to push on to the end and also wants to delay it."

—Kathleen George, *Pittsburgh Post-Gazette*

"An ambitious, lyrical exploration of the lingering wounds of the Vietnamese war . . . Butler's prose is precise, sensuous, and moving. . . . An honest and intermittently powerful attempt to find some redemptive possibilities in the lingering nightmare of that war."

—*Kirkus Reviews*

THE

DEEP

GREEN

SEA

THE

DEEP

GREEN

SEA

A Novel

Robert Olen Butler

Grove Press
New York

First published in the United States of America
by Henry Holt and Company, Inc., 1997

Printed in the United States of America
Published simultaneously in Canada

ISBN: 978-0-8021-2096-0

Grove Press
an imprint of Grove/Atlantic, Inc.
154 West 14th Street
New York, NY 10011

Distributed by Publishers Group West
www.groveatlantic.com

13 14 15 16   10 9 8 7 6 5 4 3 2 1

FOR

KELLY LEE BUTLER

THE

DEEP

GREEN

SEA

There is a moment now, come suddenly upon us, when the sound of the motorbikes from the street has faded almost to silence, and I can smell, faintly, the incense I have burned, and I am naked at last. He is naked, too, though I still have not let my eyes move beyond his face and his arms and his hands. He is very gentle, very cautious, and to my surprise, I say, "I have never done this before."

I am lying on my bed and he is beside me and we are lit by neon from the hotel across the street and he has touched only my shoulders. His hands are moving there when I say these words, and they hesitate. There is also a hesitation in me. I hear what I have said. Some place inside me says these words are true, and some other place says that I am a liar.

I am twenty-six years old and I have been with two men in my life. But I was never with them in this bed, I was never with them in this room where I was a child of my grandmother, this room where I keep the altar to my dead father, and when I removed my clothes with these men,

I did not feel I was naked with them, though I wished to
be. There was fear in my heart and incomprehension in
their eyes, and when we rose from the places where we
touched, I felt nothing except that I was alone.

Until this moment with Ben, I have known how to
understand that. I am a girl of this new Vietnam. I am not
my mother, who is of a different Vietnam and who had her
own fear and incomprehension with men, and who is far
away from me. I am alone in this world but it is all right,
I have always thought, because in a great socialist republic
everyone is equal and each of us can find a place in the
state that holds us all. There is no aloneness.

But everything is different now. I am suddenly different. I am naked. This is what I wish to tell him with my
words. It is what I wish to tell myself.

There is a surge of sound in the room, the motorbikes
again, the others going around and around the streets of
Ho Chi Minh City on a Saturday night, and I wish it was
quiet again. I want to hear the sound of his breathing. I
want to hear the faint stretching of him inside his skin as
he lifts slightly away from me in thought and turns his
head to the window.

His chest is naked and so is mine. I feel my nipples
tighten at the thought of him and I want it to be quiet
and I want the light to be better too. I want to look at his
body, this part at least. No more for now. I want to start

with this naked chest of his and also his hands, which I have been able to see for these past days but that I have not yet really looked at. I take one of these hands now in mine as he thinks about what I have said. I take it and in the cold red burning of the neon light I can see his thick hand. He worked once in the steel mills. He told me of their fire. He worked once driving a great truck many thousands of miles across his country, the United States of America, gripping the steering wheel of this truck, and I love the corded veins here as I hold his hand. "It is all right," I say. I lift his hand and put it on my chest. I cover my yearning nipple.

I look down at his hand on me and it is very large and my own hands are small and my fingers are slender and his are not, his are thick and his skin in the light from the moon and the hotel across the street seems pale and mine seems darker. I am Vietnamese. Every Vietnamese child hears the tale of how our country began. Once long ago a dragon who was the ruler of all the oceans lived in his palace in the deep deep bottom of the South China Sea. He grew very lonely, so he rose up from the sea and flew to the land, the rich jungles and mountains and plains that are now our Vietnam. And there he met a fairy princess. A very beautiful princess. And they fell in love. This is the thing that is told to us so easily and no one ever questions her mother or her grandmother or her aunt or her friend hiding with her in the dark roots of a banyan tree, even here in Saigon, the great banyan tree in the park on Dong Khoi that was there a hundred years before the revolution. I heard the story there, on the street, and you never think to ask whoever is telling you, How did this happen? How did this feeling happen between two such different creatures? My friend Diep, who was also the daughter of a prostitute, but one who did not flee, who did not give her daughter over to what she saw was a better life, my friend whispered this story to me and a stripe of light lay on her face through the cords of the roots in the banyan and she said that the fairy princess and the dragon fell in love and they married and then she laid a hundred eggs in a beautiful silk bag. And I said only, Yes, like I understood such a thing. I said, Did he love her very much? Yes, Diep said. Very Much.

And the princess had one hundred children. And there was no childhood for them. They grew instantly upon birth into very beautiful adults. Diep told me that they were both princes and princesses. Fifty boys and fifty girls. For a while they all lived together and the fairy princess was happy and the children were happy. But the dragon was not. He missed the sea and one day the fairy princess woke and he was gone. He had returned to his palace beneath the water. She understood. She tried to live on without him. But it was very difficult because she was very much in love with him. And so she called him back. I do not know how. I did not think to ask. Somehow he knew to come back and yet he could not stay. He told her that their differences were too great. He could not be happy in the land. He had to return to his palace, though he promised that if she ever knew any danger or terrible hardship he would come back to help. So he took fifty of their children with him and he returned to the sea. And she took fifty of their children with her to the mountains. And these children became the people of Vietnam.

It seemed a very beautiful sad story to me. And I came home to the very room that I lie in with this man. Years ago in this place I came home to my grandmother and I told her the story and she said that it was true.

No. Not my grandmother. She and I lived in this room for most of the time I was a child. But I heard about the dragon and the fairy princess before that. I came to my mother, and that was near to this place but not in this room, and I was perhaps seven years old, and I told her the story and she said it was true. But she corrected one thing. They were all sons. A hundred sons. And the eldest of them became the first king of Vietnam. I did not ask anything more, questions I now have that roll in me and break in me more strongly than the waves of the dragon's precious sea. It is this that I wonder as I hold this man's hand in my bed: how did she look upon her dragon when she first lay with him? Did the princess take the great scaled hand of this creature that she was loving so strongly even then, ready as she was to open her body to him, did she put her tiny, silken hands on his and did she pass her fingers softly over the layers of his hard flesh still smelling of the sea, did she touch the tips of his claws, did she look into his great red eyes and see all the gentleness that she had dreamed for? And surely the answer is yes. Surely that is what she did.

I cannot see Ben's eyes. Not the color of them. Not what might be there of his heart. He turns his face to me when I lead him to touch my breast and there is only shadow where his eyes are and I cannot see. But I feel him through his hand. He is very gentle in this place of steel mills and trucks and I know he likes the touch of me and I know this even though he lifts his hand now. Just the tiniest bit so that he does not touch me with his flesh, but I can still feel the heat of him. "Are you sure?" he says. He believes this thing I have said about myself. I believe it, too. And I am sure of this: with this man, I am naked and I do not feel as if I am alone. "Yes," I say, and he puts his hand on me but not over my nipple. He puts his hand in the center of my chest, between my breasts, and the tip of his middle finger is in the hollow of my throat. It feels as if he touches my whole body with his palm and I do not know what is to come and I tell myself I do not care.

She tells me I'm the first man she's ever done it with and I stop right off. It wouldn't make a difference in my feelings for her, either way, but when she says she's never made love before, I do feel like I've been given some kind of a second chance. I almost tell her it's the same for me. For Christ's sake, to be able to start again from a place where there's nothing to remember, nothing to ask about, nothing but what's there for both of you right in that moment, without any history at all, that's almost too good to be true. And to my surprise, my face goes hot and I get a feeling in my eyes like when you step in front of a coke oven and you take that first blast of heat before you start shoveling the spill.

Like that maybe, like a feeling at the mill, but that's a little bit of bullshit on my part. In fact, it's like when you're about to cry. This woman lying here in a dim room saying she's a virgin and she wants me to be inside her body and she is who she is, she listens to me talk like she does with those sweet dark eyes never looking away even for a second and she takes me into a room like this and says so easily this is my good luck Buddha and this is my long life Buddha and this is my ancestor shrine and it's like she thinks I'm going to understand these things right off. She just makes me part of them, though a couple of the things should seem silly to me, little ceramic fat guys sitting on the floor, but I don't want to laugh at them, only maybe a quiet laugh in pleasure from her being like this. A Vietnam woman. In a room in goddamn Saigon, after all. Those people out there going around and around all night on their motorcycles, a bunch of them maybe guys who twenty years ago were in the business of killing Americans. And she tells me that there is no past at all and she wants me and I feel like I'm going to goddamn cry.

So I turn my face to the window. And I hope that it will be all right for her. I hope she shouldn't be waiting for the man she's going to marry, though it's not like I've ruled out that the man she could marry is me. If I figured otherwise, I think I'd be strong enough to get up and thank her as sweetly as I could so it wouldn't hurt her and I'd get the hell out of here. But I realize—and this is a shock to me, as a matter of fact—that it could be me. It took me to come back to the fucking Nam to realize that I could be married to somebody again. And just at the moment I come to the little shock of that, Tien says, "It is all right," and she takes my hand and puts it on her breast.

This is the first real touch. The first touch of sex. We're half naked at the moment and we've been kissing, but this is the first touch. I take my hand away but not very far. I can't say that something's warning me. I just want to be sure she isn't making a mistake about what she wants. They think about these things a little different over here. Even if the communists are in control, they still seem to think in some older ways. I don't want her to end up convinced she's spoiled for some other man, just in case. Though I'm wanting to go on with this very bad now. And it's been a long time since I've felt this way. I don't even try to think of the last time. I lift my hand just a little bit and my palm is burning with the tiny hard spot where the tip of her nipple was and what I do think of is a moment when I was pulling oil on the California coast, some years ago now, and I stepped out of my rig in a rest stop somewhere in the San Joaquin Valley and it was night and the air was full of the smell of oranges. A couple of Peterbilts had just huffed away and they'd been full of oranges and the smell was everywhere, that and the smell of diesel fuel, and I suddenly wanted a woman bad. I wasn't sure why but it seemed to have something to do with this place. Saigon. These streets are always full of that kind of mix of smells, some sweet something, fruit or flowers or incense, but something else too in the same air, dry rot or old fish or the exhaust from the motor-bikes. I got out of my truck, and what passed for a mar-riage in my life was dead already and I didn't care if my pecker ever saw the light of day again and it was a thing that smelled like Vietnam that made me want a woman once more.

I push Tien a little bit. "Are you sure you want to?" I ask her and I hope the answer is going to be yes. And it is. She says it right away and I put my hand in the center of her chest and I wish my hand is big enough to hold her in it, all of her, just cover her with the palm of my hand and keep her safe and make her happy. I ache in the shoulders from wanting that. And the mix of things is in the air right then. The incense from her ancestor shrine and the smell of all the cheap motors outside and somebody in a room nearby cooking with the fish oil they use.

Soon after I got back here to Vietnam I came to this street I once knew. It was the only one that stuck in my head after all these years. And that was because of a woman. I guess we used the word *love* to each other for a few months, her and me. Whatever love was for me at twenty. And there was something between us for a while. Something. But I didn't come back here looking for her. It was just a street I knew. There were bars along here, in 1966. A clothing shop now. A noodle shop. A place on the sidewalk fixing tires. Just a street with its life out in the open like life in this city always seemed to be and it still is and I walked around here and I sat at a tiny plastic table in the open garage mouth of the noodle shop and I drank a warm Coke, staying away from the ice, and this was all I had to worry about now, the water, and I watched these people moving around and I just held still knowing that I didn't have to be afraid about Vietnam anymore.

The water and the dogs. They always shy away as if every one of them has been beaten since birth, but I don't trust them. They're slick-featured, scoop-eared, more like dingoes or hyenas than like American dogs and while I was sitting there on that first day at the noodle shop, one of them sniffed by, stopping at a stain on the sidewalk and then he saw me watching him and he flinched back right away, ducking his head like I'd raised my hand to hit him. I was thinking I shouldn't have this feeling. He'd just had it bad as a pup and I sucked back my nerves and clicked at him a little bit. He stopped at this but he was clearly not going to come to me. "Be careful of all the dogs," a voice said and I looked up into her face.

That first moment I saw her, I flinched a little inside, her face was so beautiful. And like with all these Vietnamese, it surprised me. There's always something floating in a Vietnamese face that you don't expect. There was an old woman with her gums red from chewing betel leaves who'd been crouching for a long while off to my left, drinking her soup with her bowl up at her face the whole time, but once, she'd glanced over to me, just a couple of minutes before I clicked at the dog and started all this, and she smiled her bright red smile and she had a color in her eyes like when the interstate ahead looks like water and is reflecting the sky. Wet and almost blue but dark from concrete. And I thought when I saw the mama-san's eyes that her daddy was French or something. So when there was this beautiful face before me telling me to be careful of the dogs, I wasn't surprised by the things you didn't expect in it. Her eyes were very dark but they weren't so sharply lidded. They looked soft around the edge and her face wasn't so round. She had a squareness to her jaw and a mouth that smiled now a little bit but just on one side and her skin was pale and I just eased back and thought, Holy shit this is a beautiful woman, and she said, "They might be sick." She'd been talking English, too, with not much of an accent at all.

"Thanks," I said, and she was moving off. Just like that. Nothing more. She was through a passageway a couple of storefronts down and gone and I sat there wondering what the hell just happened. I looked over to where the dog was and he'd taken off. I thought about standing up, about walking down to the passageway and at least look-ing along to where this woman disappeared, but I didn't. The mama-san was gone too. There was the buzz and rush of motorcycles in the street, of course, and people crouching on the sidewalk in either direction, but it was the time of day in Saigon when if you're on foot, you find some shade and stay still and nobody was near me or coming toward me and for a moment I felt absolutely alone. In the midst of this city of all places, I felt invisible, and that was a feeling I realized I wanted to hold on to for a while and so I didn't get up. I let her face fade and I waited and I even closed my eyes.

Then there was a car horn close by. I opened my eyes and at the curb was a Renault with a Saigontourist decal across its back window and I knew she was going to appear again. And she did. Out of that passageway and across the sidewalk and into the car and she didn't even give me another glance. So I thought, That's the end of it. But a week later I have my hand on her naked chest and she says yes it's okay and I still don't move. This time, it's from sitting there and wondering at the switchback my luck just seemed to take.

He does not move his hand when I tell him it is okay. I am ready for this moment, but he is waiting. I like this about him. He will be very gentle with me. Very slow. I listen to hear him breathe. There are still too many night sounds and I tell him, "Bring your face close to mine, please."

This makes him cock his head, like he has not understood. "Bring your face close," I say and he does, sliding to

me, and he thinks I want him to kiss me and I say, when
he is very near, when his breath has touched my cheek,
"Just there. For a moment wait please. I want to know
that you are real." He waits. He is real. I can feel his
breath on me.

On the day I first saw him, I would not look at him
a second time. Not straight at him. But I glanced in the
rearview mirror as the car pulled away. I am a careful girl.
I already acted a different way from who I am by finding
some American man sitting almost directly beneath my
window and speaking to him, even if it was for his own
good. Now I could only see him again in a mirror, like
the American legend I read, a story about a man and a
woman with snakes for hair who could turn him to stone
if he looked at her directly. And his face was turned this
way and I wondered if he could see me watch him in this
small mirror and so I looked for the dog. I feared this
man might try to touch it and he would be hurt. I saw no
dog and I thought that I was not really so very interested
in where the dog was, and when the car began to move
and the man's face was gone, I was a little bit angry with
myself for my shyness.

But I am not shy when he brings his face close to mine
in my bed. I feel his breath on me and I pull back just a
little bit to see him clearly. His eyes are very dark, like
a Vietnamese, I think. And I am reminded of the dragon

once more. There are many straight lines in the face of a dragon, square corners. Ben's face has much of this in it. At the bottom of his face, at his jaw, there is a squareness that I think is like a dragon's head. I am still trying to understand the story I learned from my friend inside the banyan tree. For a moment I try to see the terribleness of such a face as beautiful. I mean by this, the dragon's face. When I feel Ben's breath and he becomes real and when I know that this real man is about to put his hands on me and his mouth and all the secret parts of him, I do not find him terrible. But I think he can help me understand, because on this night there is something inside me that is afraid, and this is in the same moment with some other thing inside me that wants to reach to him and to put my hand behind his head and pull him to me.

I tell myself, the fairy princess loved the dragon. She loved him. There are things that frighten us for a while and then from the very strong feeling of this fear we find a different strong feeling. I lived sometimes in a room not far from this one. I was still with my mother and it was on the nights when she did not leave me with my grandmother. I know now that these were the times when there was no all-night man from the bar where she worked. Some man may be there in the afternoon, but she did not lie naked with him through the long night till the morning, and it was those times she kept me on a pallet nearby.

And when it was the rainy season I woke from the sound of thunder. The storms came in and bellowed in the air and I heard them with my ears but I felt them inside my body also, each cry. And for a few years it was like this. The cry of the thunder would carry me into my mother's bed on the nights when there was no one else and she would hold me in her arms.

Sometimes the bed smelled very strange to me, not the smell of my mother at all, something wet, a little like the rain that was rushing outside but stronger, thicker, a smell more like brine, like the sea. For a while I wondered if she was loved by a dragon. The thunder would beat at my body and this smell was in me and my mother was naked beneath the thin silk robe she wore and she held me close and I dreamed of the dragon rising from the South China Sea and flying to my mother and loving her in some way that I did not understand and then he went up into the sky because his kingdom needed him and he did not want to go but he had no choice and he rose high into the air and he cried out his pain and she felt it in her body and I felt it in my body and the dragon cast the sea down upon us to remind my mother of his love and he flew away. And so I came to love the thunder. On the nights I was with my mother, I went to the window at this call and I opened the shutter and I let the sound take me in its hands and squeeze me until I grew wet from the rain and my mother would draw me away. In jealousy, I thought. And when my mother was gone away and the rockets brought another thunder to Saigon, I would go to the windows and the sky was red and my grandmother would pull me away and tell me that there was something dangerous out there. But I still loved the sound. I loved this thing I once had feared.

I lift my hand and I put it at the back of Ben's head and he is not wet from the sea and his flesh is not hard scaled. He is soft. His hair is soft and I let my fingers slide inside his hair and I pull him to me and he does not rush, he lets me draw him to me as slow as I wish. Then his breath is on my face and then his lips touch mine.

I have known other kisses. A boy, dim now in my mind, in those dark early years of our socialist republic, and I was sixteen and he was a guard at Reunification Hall, and he wore a uniform the color of a tree gecko, and we treaded on each other as lightly as that, like lizards. And there was Mr. Bao, who was a driver for a while at Saigontourist. He asked me one night to go to a theater that plays movies from America. It is in a long room with a distant screen and it is very dark. He asked me to go to this place because Elizabeth Taylor and Paul Newman would he there in a movie called *Cat on a Hot Tin Roof*. He did not speak good English and he wanted me to tell him the meaning of this title. I did not know. It was not an idiom I had studied. I said that it must be some American legend that would be made clear in the movie.

It was so dark we could not see to move once the movie began, but all around us, there were couples kissing. This is the only place in public in our city where this is possible. On the screen was a woman's voice translating all of the speaking in the film into Vietnamese, for all the characters, both men and women. I could hear only a murmur of Elizabeth Taylor and Paul Newman speaking beneath this one female voice. I tried hard to listen to the American voices, but I could make out none of their words. I grew angry at the very sound of my own language. I should have felt shame at this, I think. But I cared only for these Americans on the screen. I grew more ashamed, conscious now of my secret attachment to these people. But Elizabeth Taylor was very beautiful and her husband was very harsh with her and I was concerned. He did not wish to touch her, in spite of her beauty. And he also was very angry at his father. The father wanted very much to please his son. He tried hard, I think. He was there in a great house with his son, alive, and he was trying hard, and I grew very angry at Paul Newman for not understanding.

These thoughts were in me when Mr. Bao's hand came and turned my face to him and he put his lips on mine. At the touch of his lips, I felt only a hard little knot in my chest. I pulled back. He said he was sorry and I said that it was okay and we both looked at the screen. I wanted to jump up from my seat and scream at Paul Newman to go to his father and embrace him. He is your father, I would cry, you should be grateful to have his love. And then I would tell Paul Newman to go to his wife and do what she desires. People should touch when they are in need. And I heard these words in my head and I felt Elizabeth Taylor's pain as my own and I looked toward the darkness where Mr. Bao was sitting, hurting still from my coldness.

And so I took my hand and I turned his face to me once again and we kissed some more, though I wondered at this thing, why people sought it so, and then time went on from that night, and eventually we were in the bed in his rooms, and with each touch between us, the thing I wanted so much to feel murmured beneath our acts like the voices of the American actors in the movie, saying things I wanted to hear but being drowned out by this other, too-familiar voice. And I lay beside Mr. Bao afterwards, and all the voices were silent, and when he coughed softly I was startled, because I had forgotten that he was there.

So I rose up from that bed and left Mr. Bao and after that I have not touched a man. I have been free to do so. But I have chosen not to. I have taken my place in the state, working for Saigontourist to show the truth of how we live to those from other countries that come here. And until this moment, this is how I live. When I do not work, I have some girlfriends and we go to a movie or to a park or to a restaurant or to karaoke or to the show at the theater that was once the French Opera House and was then the national assembly building of the puppet government of the divided Vietnam. Or I sit alone in this room and I read a book or I listen on the radio to the classic Vietnam opera or I say prayers and light incense for the soul of my father.

These prayers I say every night. I am a modern girl of a great socialist state but I am not a communist. Not so very many Vietnamese are communists. I can still pray for the spirits of the dead like my mother and my grandmother taught me. I pray for my grandmother, too, but the ancestor shrine that sits against the wall next to the window has one careful purpose and that is to receive the prayers for the soul of my father, a soul that I have always understood to be suffering terribly in the next life and in great need of these things I offer him.

And when I lie down in my bed and it is night, there is still the smell in the air of the incense I have burned for him. I lie in my bed and sometimes I wear a silk robe and sometimes I am naked. I lie in my bed for all these years that I have been in this room as a woman, and I always lie alone until this night when Ben touches me for the first time. But it was not clear to me how alone this was until Ben came to me. I did not feel how painful all the nights without him have been until he was here. This is a strange thing to me. As Ben kisses me and I feel he is here with me and I feel that no one has ever been here until this moment, I think that perhaps my father has always protected me from that pain. Perhaps what I gave to my father's soul, the company of my prayers, he always gave back to me. This is what I think as Ben kisses me. And I may seem shy still, as I think too much of Mr. Bao and Elizabeth Taylor and my friends who go with me to restaurants and fill the air with empty words, and I do not concentrate on the feeling of his lips on mine. But it is not shyness. There is at this moment the smell of incense in my room. His lips are upon me and I smell the smoke of my father's soul.

My first time in this room, she asked me if I could wait for a few minutes. She said it was her custom to pray at a certain moment of the day, as soon as she came home, and she felt that the soul who was in her care knew that. "He is waiting," she said.

"Of course," I said. I didn't mention it at the time hut I was just happy to be here with her in a private place at last. She could do what she wanted, if she'd just let me hang around her.

There wasn't much furniture. It would have been a natural thing for me to sit on the bed to wait, but I didn't. I sat on a straw mat instead, before a low, black lacquer table with inlaid white cranes.

We'd just spent the day together. The previous afternoon I'd waited in front of the noodle shop to catch sight of her again, and the Saigontourist car finally arrived. She got out, dressed in the same white blouse with a big bow at the throat and tight skirt cut down to her knees that she'd worn the day before. She was clearly a guide of some sort. I'd been waiting a long time and I was caught off guard now. She was going to dash across the sidewalk and disappear before I could even rise to my feet. But she saw me and hesitated. She looked over her shoulder—I think to see if the car was gone, and it was. Then she came toward me. I stood up.

"I've been staying away from the dogs," I said.

"Good," she said. "But you came back here."

"Yes."

"Is this place in the guidebooks now? I have thought it is a place where only a Vietnamese would eat."

"Oh, it's very good," I said. I tried to read her tone. Did she know I was waiting for her and she was flattered and was flirting with me? But I couldn't catch that in her voice. It almost sounded as if she was really trying to get a fix on this noodle shop.

Then she asked, "Was it a coincidence that you are here when I am coming home from work?" She was still deadpan. I was very conscious of her being a young woman working for a communist government. But her eyes were bright and they seemed happy to stay fixed on me.

"Did I look surprised to see you?"

She wrinkled her brow at this, trying to remember. "I should have noticed that. I might figure you out without even asking."

I said, "I don't think I looked surprised."

She nodded and her eyes didn't leave me. "Is there some other sign I should be seeing?"

"I've been here about three hours. But that wouldn't show."

She looked past me to the little table where I'd been sitting. There were half a dozen empty bottles. Three beers, three Cokes. I'd started with the beer, but I didn't want a buzz on when I saw her again. I wanted to have a clear head for her.

"Yes. Maybe it shows," she said.

I wanted to explain about the beers, but I just felt myself grinning at her like a fool. It was clear to me now that, deadpan though she was, she was playing with me, and I wanted to keep that going. But all I could think of was something sincere. I said, "I wanted to see you again."

This made her eyes break with me. She looked down, her face dipped, and I thought I'd made a bad mistake. But she came back to me. Only a moment later she came back. Her eyes were on mine again and she said, "Why is that? There are many girls in Ho Chi Minh City for you to look at."

I had no answer for that question. She was right, of course. But it had never really been like that for me in my life, always flashing on some woman or other, instantly, though if you believed most of the guys I've been around, that's the way the world works. And there was something there between this woman and me, even as we stood on the sidewalk in front of the noodle shop talking around it. There was something right away, and somehow our eyes knew it while our brains didn't. Finally I said, "No one else cared about saving me from the dogs."

She smiled that sweet half-smile from the day before and she said, "It was my civic duty."

"Have you warned many men about the dogs of Saigon?"

This stopped her. It seemed to me that she was having the same trouble I'd just had in answering. After a moment she said, simply, "No."

"Why is that?" I asked. "There are many men in Saigon who could be in peril."

"No one else calls to the dogs like they are worth loving."

"So there were reasons for both of us."

"Yes."

I was stuck now. I shuffled around and tried to think of something to suggest. "I'd like to take you somewhere. For noodles, maybe. I know a great place." I gestured at the shop behind me.

She laughed briefly, softly, at this, but then her face went suddenly serious. She said, "It is not so easy."

"Because you don't know my name. I'm Benjamin Cole. The short name is Ben."

"I am Le Thi Tien. My given name is Tien." She held out her hand and I took it and she had a firm grip and we shook and let our hands go and I thought we both were happy to have touched in this clear and strong way. Then she said, "But that does not fix the difficult thing. My work for Saigontourist means I should not fraternize in public with someone who looks like a guest of our country."

"Then let me hire you." These words were out of my mouth before I could think about them.

He looked very concerned suddenly and I was sure it was because of the words he spoke, though I had not heard them at first in the way he feared. And that was an interesting thing. In the next moment, when I thought of him liking me and then hiring me and I finally saw what he was feeling bad about, I still was not hurt. I was not my mother. He was not a GI. Though he was American. Obviously so. And I had my own concern now. I wanted to do this in the way he had first imagined. I wanted to sit in a noodle shop with him in my softest silk dress, with my throat naked and my knees bared, I wanted to speak with him and watch his gentleness reach out to the ragged dogs that went by. This desire surprised me, and it seemed an impossible thing.

But there was this offer. I said, "I could take you on a tour of the city tomorrow."

"Good," he said. "Yes."

And that is what we did. With my driver Mr. Thu we went to the Giac Lam Pagoda, the oldest in Ho Chi Minh City, built in 1744, and to the Reunification Hall, which had been the evil Nguyen Van Thieu's palace and where our triumphant revolutionary forces first unfurled our flag, and to the Ben Thanh Market, where it is clear how plentiful consumer goods are in our country, and I spoke like a person who had never worn a silk dress in her life and had never shown her knees, and Ben was mostly quiet and he was very respectful of me and our position in public, even when Mr. Thu was waiting in the car and Ben and I were alone walking in the close and steamy aisles of the market full of jackfruit and alligator pears and bitter melons and squash and green peppers and bins of rice and stacks of dried fish and cages of ducks and chickens, or when we were alone in a cloud of incense with the Lady Buddha nearby, a dozen faces piled on her head and a thousand hands surrounding her, each with an eye in its palm, or when we stood on the balcony where our revolutionary flag first flew and no one was there but the two of us. Even in those moments, Ben was quiet and I filled the air with words I knew by heart but suddenly could barely recognize.

Then we were standing before the War Crimes Museum. It is in an old French colonial compound beneath beautiful tamarind trees and Mr. Thu was once again in the car and Ben and I were standing on the sidewalk. Ben had not spoken in a long time. He waited for me to show him to the ticket kiosk, which was before us, and beyond was the courtyard where American tanks and armored vehicles sat and also a French guillotine, and inside the building were rooms filled with photos of dead women and children, and already my head was swarming with words. I did not listen to them. I could not move.

Finally he said, very softly, very near my ear, I thought, though I did not turn to see, "I don't think this is having the same effect as a meal in a noodle shop."

"No," I said. "I have not spoken a word of my own all day." Now I turned to him. He had pulled back from me and was peering ahead, into the courtyard. I said, "Do you understand that?"

He looked at me. "Understand?"

"Do you understand that all these words have not been mine?"

"That was my point about the noodles."

"But I cannot be myself in a restaurant, either. I would worry about the thoughts of those around us."

His shoulders lifted and fell, only slightly, quite slowly. He had sighed. I had not heard it, but I knew. A strange alertness had come upon me with him and it was not a pleasant thing, really. But I knew that was because of this public sidewalk and the bow at my throat and the impossibility of my reaching out now and taking his hand.

With the sigh still lingering in his voice, he said, "What are we going to do, Tien? Should I just go back to my hotel and never bother you again?"

"No," I said, and the word came out sharp and quick, and I thought that finally on this day I had said a word of my own. I said it again. "No." And then I said, "I am glad we have met. I will arrange something."

Then I lied to Mr. Thu, telling him that Ben was thinking of moving to the Metropole. Mr. Thu is a young man with a wife and children of his own, not from the generation who suffered so very much in the war, and I thought perhaps he would understand anyway. But for this day I left it with a lie, and he dropped Ben and me at the Metropole, which is the hotel just across the street from my apartment, and I told him the American would arrange the transfer of his lodging on his own and I would go home for the day, for it was late afternoon.

Mr. Thu drove off, and in the shadow of the Metropole, Ben looked around and across the side street and he realized where we were. "Noodles," he said.

"Tea," I said. "You can go with me and I will make you some very nice tea."

"And what about your neighbors?"

"That is not a public thing," I said, and though what I said was true in a way, it was also true that I was finally prepared to accept some censure for this man.

He nodded at this with a soft smile and perhaps he understood, perhaps he had grown very alert about me, as well.

And so at last I found myself sitting on a straw mat before a lacquer table in Tien's apartment and she disappeared into her little bathroom. She hadn't made any gesture toward it, but I knew the place where she'd do her prayers. On the opposite wall from where I sat was a little table. It was spread with a white cloth and there were two narrow brass holders with blue irises drooping in them and a plate of fruit, a couple of mangoes, the yellow of them dark-spotted from ripeness, a bunch of the tiny bananas that are so impossibly sweet, also going dark, and in the center of the table was a glass bowl with sand holding a cluster of incense sticks. I'd seen this kind of thing before. In another little room somewhere not much farther down this back alley. With a woman who was as young as me at the time. And, I always thought, just about as scared.

As I waited for Tien to appear again, I tried to see Kim's face in my mind. Her eyes came, large but cut deep in her face like they were done fast. The eyes of these people in the Nam. It was the one thing about them you never quite stopped noticing. The one thing that kept saying they were from some very different place. Not that I minded Kim's eyes. They were beautiful, and though I was scared shitless about half the time in Nam, I was also happy to be away from Wabash, I think, which was my home, a little Illinois steel mill town in the bottomland of the Mississippi River across from St. Louis. I was happy she was different. But all these years later, that was all I could see of her easily, the thing that wasn't like anything else I knew.

I tried briefly to picture Kim in some particular moment, and since I was staring at this prayer table I thought of her at her own place where she took care of a soul. But she was across the room. I was on the bed and she was far away and there was another face instead. A large photo sat in the middle of the table, an old man with a brimless little mandarin hat. Kim's grandfather, I think.

The bathroom door opened and Tien stepped out. She'd gone in wearing that white blouse and long-cut skirt from Saigontourist. Now she was in black silk, a blouse and pants that rippled around her and made me want to touch her already, made me want to forget the things I knew I had to be with her, like careful and slow. Her hair was down now. It was very long and black like the world beyond the push of my headlights. She said, "Just a little while."

"Yes," I said, though I could hardly make a sound.

She moved to the table and knelt there and her bare feet lay beneath her bottom, her toes in a fine little row, and this was going to be tough, I knew. She lifted her face to the table and I realized now that something was missing. There was no photo. I'd learned enough from Kim to know this was odd.

But how little there is from Kim. How little that comes easily. She crouched before her grandfather and she prayed and the smoke rose from her hands and filled the room with the smell of something, maybe jasmine. I can't remember exactly, but how else would I know this smell? I love the smells of things. The smell of oranges in the San Joaquin Valley. I remember that moment, though it was a time without love, without a woman nearby who would soon come to me and touch me. The smell of the land on the long runs out of St. Louis, the earth turned out there in the dark, ready for seed. Even the smell of the mill. The naphtha and the coke gas. I loved that smell like my father loved it. My own dead. He'd come home from his shift and he'd smell like those mill smells, and also like Lava soap and the starch of his off-work shirt. If his spirit is caught somewhere without the prayers of his kin, like the Vietnamese believe, it's out there haunting Wabash Steel, out at the blast furnace or maybe the field next to it, where he'd lift me and put me on his shoulders and he'd think for a long time and stay quiet and he'd fill himself with the smell, now and then, his chest lifting and he'd take it all in and I would too. That I remember. He'd take it all in and he'd point to the thin stack rising near the highway and at its top was a vivid, gelatinous flame thrashing there and he'd say, That's the bleeder valve. Look how beautiful the flame is. And I would look and it was very beautiful. And I squeeze hard at these things I still have of Kim. Things come and I don't know if they are memories or things I'm dreaming, making up from some deep and persuasive place. Her smell. Her hair smelled of the incense. She'd come to me from her dead grandfather and she was naked and her body was slick and hard and she'd lay me on my back and crouch over me and when I was inside her she would lean forward and her hair would fall on my face and I would smell the incense, like I was being taken up in her prayer.

Then her face slid up to mine and she kissed me with loud smacks and she moved on me and she whispered, "You like Kim very many."

"Much," I whispered. We'd played this little game before. She'd made the mistake the first night I'd met her at the bar and she'd thought about it when I corrected her and then she let it go, but we played it out to a new conclusion the first time we made love and every time since. I'd say, "I like Kim very much."

"Many," she'd say. "One hundred times."

And I should remember that first time, because Kim was the first woman I ever made love to. There was a girl in a trailer park in Wabash, out past the blast furnace, and she had buck teeth and a squint and a wonderful body and we touched one night in the dark and the smell of the mill was very strong. She said she was a good girl, not to forget that, and I said I wouldn't, though I avoided her after that night. I was never inside her, though she touched me with her hand and she asked me to touch her and I said, "No, I'm sorry." I'd heard about a woman's smell from the other guys and I was afraid of it and I couldn't look at her after that night. Her name is gone now, but it might have been Jasmine. That might be where the smell of the incense is really from in this thing that comes to me like a memory. And I can't think of the first time with Kim, exactly. The night was very dark. There was no incense. There's nothing of that night. Just later, when there was the smoke in her hair and the prayers for the dead.

And even then, what was the big feeling I was supposed to have? What was this thing that people say makes you so close, you and a woman? I kept looking for something important from all that and it stumped me. Though I never fit in with the others who lived over the road. I'd hit the truck stops and I'd park my rig off a ways from the others and I'd find a place in the restaurant alone, the last table on the way to the shower stalls or the pinball machines, and I'd stay there out of the traffic. But sometimes when they'd talk about all this and it was just fuck this one and fuck that one and go to this truck stop in Indiana and they sit buck naked on your table and ain't that the life, I'd wonder if maybe they were basically right. If that's all it came down to.

I try not to think like all those guys I spent too many years with in the mills or on the roads. No, I don't mean all the guys. Just the noisy ones. There were others like me, I think. I try not to let myself sound like the noisy ones. There's enough of my mama in me to give me another way of looking at things. She's another one of my dead. Her spirit's probably in the Wabash Public Library with the copper bust of Andrew Carnegie inside the front door and the floors wide and scuffed and the fans going in the corners and the smell of old books. She'd bring me there and she'd get her books and she'd read at night when my dad was working a late shift and she'd weep sometimes and she'd laugh sometimes and I've done some reading but not near as much as she'd wanted for me. I still like the smell of a book, though. I'll find a few old books in some thrift store in some little town somewhere in this last couple of years since I've been off the road and just moving around, and I'll pick one up and put my face in the pages and smell it.

I wonder sometimes if my mom and dad had a big feeling when they touched. There was a lot of pain with all that, I think. They lost a little girl quite a few years before

I was born and it was hard on them, I'm pretty sure. Then they had me late. But I'd also find them touching each other. I have one moment in my head from a night when I woke up from something and it was when my dad was working nights and I got out of bed and the house was quiet but the lights were still on. I expected to find my mama reading. She wasn't in our little front room and I went on to the kitchen and I stood quiet in the door and my dad was sitting on a kitchen chair with his shirt off. He was just home and he was sitting with his forearms over his thighs and slumped a little bit forward and my mama was standing behind him and touching his back. Not a back rub. Much lighter. Just slowly sweeping his back with her fingertips and his head was bowed and once, when her hand went up to his shoulder, his own hand rose suddenly and their fingertips met.

Like that, maybe. It's supposed to happen like that. But I can't remember a touch like that with Kim. There was some cute talk. There was her hair falling on me. There was the thing that happened for me when I was inside her, a thing that the guys in the stops have some words for. But I can't quite hear it in those ways. I mean that moment when I run inside her, when I run like it feels when I'm on a good rig and I'm coming out of the hills after a slow climb and I crest and suddenly I think I'm falling. But that's not really a good moment I'm talking about. Most of the time you feel like you and the truck are pretty much together. But in that sudden run, you feel like you've broken away from this thing you're riding. You have nothing to do with it and sometimes that scares you a little and sometimes it just makes you feel like you've flown off to someplace else and you're not sure where that is.

The place wasn't with Kim, though. I went home from the war in February of 1967, and for a few months before that, I didn't even see her. I went home and that meant Wabash and I went back to my room in the little brick house on Hagemeyer Avenue where I still had baseball cards and my steel-toed shoes and some shirts in a closet that were the color of the deuce-and-a-halfs I'd just driven for a year and were still smelling like the mill. I went there and I slept till noon every day for three months and I went out until I found Mattie from Wabash High who I always liked to look at and she remembered me and she was a waitress at the Woolworth's and she didn't ask me any questions at that time and we got married and I lay in another room on the same street, with her, and she was tall, and though she was lanky, there seemed to be so much of her when she was naked, and she seemed soft to the touch, and she had heavy eyebrows and hair she kept rolled tight in a lace net when she was working but she let it down for me long and straight. That should have been

what I needed. That should have been what I'd been waiting for all along and I should have gotten back on at the
mill like my dad wanted me to do now that I was home
from a war, but it never quite turned out that way.

There was nothing even like the moment when Tien
rose from her prayers when she brought me to her room
and was not ready for us to touch. There would be no
touching and I knew it and still there'd never been a
moment for me like when I sat on her straw mat and she
turned to me and I was having trouble taking a breath
with her hair down for me this first time like it was. I sat
on the straw mat and she turned to me and behind her
the smoke rose from the incense she'd lit, dark, without a
flame, and her hair was coming down a little bit over one
shoulder and she smiled at me and I said, "Why is there
no picture?"

He surprised me when he knew about the ancestors. He
asked me why I did not have a photo on my shrine and I
think I acted in a strange way then. I had known for many
years that someone would someday ask me questions. For
too many years I waited for questions with fear in my
heart, but no one said anything. I was the orphan daughter who lived with her grandmother and I knew all that I

should say at school and my grandmother knew whatever she knew to say and you could not tell any other story from looking at my face.

I said to him, "I will make the tea now."

He is a good man. A careful man. He said, "That would be fine."

I went about the task that my hands know so well. But there were so many things in my head. My memories. As they have always been, some are clear. Some are not. My mother is clear, in a certain way. I thought of her while I made the tea. I lay with her sometimes and we slept and I do not remember when was the first time I asked the question. Maybe I never did ask about my father. Maybe this was a thing that she told me before I ever had a chance to notice. My father was a soldier and he was dead in the war. This was all there was for me to know. And she would cry very quickly about this and there were many tears and I did not try to know more. But once, I asked her why only Grandfather's picture was on her ancestor shrine and she said that there were no photos of my father. I did not ask another why. She had not yet begun to cry and I stopped before she did.

Then there was one night, and it was near the end of things. The liberators—though I did not think of them in that way then; I was a child and my mother was a bargirl—the liberators were very near and there were many rockets falling into the city. So there were no men coming to her bed and I was beside her. I could smell only her on that night, nothing of the sea. She smelled good and I told her so and she said it was a soap that came from America. It was 99 and 44 one-hundreds percent pure, she said, like me, her sweet daughter. I pressed closer to her, at her side, and her arm came around me. I wondered for a moment what it was in me that I was not one hundred percent pure and I thought to ask her. But before I did, she said that I could stay a good girl even without a daddy.

He was on her mind that night. She wanted to speak of him and I waited and I was glad, I think, to hear whatever she might say. My friend who told me of the dragon and the princess and whose mother also worked in bars was very proud that she was the daughter of a Vietnamese colonel. And though he had not married her mother and had now gone far away, he'd taken my friend once to the beach at Vung Tau. Since all I really knew was that my father was dead, my friend said things that I did not like. She said that my father was probably some man who came to the bar. She touched my face and turned it one way and then another and she said that he might be an American. I had already heard some things about how babies are made, mostly from Diep herself, but I had not grasped it yet really and I was not entirely sure why she looked for this in my face, and I slapped her hand away and I went home, and that night I wanted to ask my mother if my father was an American from the bar. But I was with my grandmother instead and I asked her. I told how Diep had looked at me and said this thing. So my grandmother put her hand on my shoulder and took me to the mirror and her face hovered over mine there. This is Tien, she said. Then she gently drew away from me and only my face was in the mirror. Is there anyone else that you see? she asked.

I tried. I had no answer yet if he was a Vietnamese man or an American man and I did not yet know why he would show in my face, but I looked and I saw only what I had always seen. No, I said. And I stood there and looked at myself and my grandmother was nearby. I could feel her there for a few moments and then she was gone and I watched my own face watching me and I found I did not have any more questions.

But on that night in April of 1975, when my mother already had secretly decided to go away from me forever—so that I could live a better life in the new Vietnam—I understand that—and so that she could live at all, believing as she did all the slanders about what the new government would do to a prostitute for the Americans—I understand all of this—on that night, she had to explain more about my father. I think my

grandmother made her do this. My grandmother must
have known of her plans by then and though she taught
me that I am myself and that I am alone, she also wanted
me to know the truth about this from my own mother.
What hard words must have passed between them that I
never heard.

My darling, my mother said to me, your father is dead.
Do not forget that.

I am certain that is what she said. Whenever I have
remembered this as an adult she sounds a little bit crazy.
She was, I suppose. In ways that at eight years old I could
not see.

I know he is dead, I said to her, and she must have heard
the tears in my voice because she sat up and turned to
see me and there was still a lamp burning nearby and I
could see her face and I looked hard there for something
of myself. I remembered my face in Grandmother's mirror
and I wanted to see if there was something of my mother
clear in me. I was not sure. She was blurred now with my
tears and what I saw mostly in her face was the squeeze of
a feeling that I had never seen in anyone's face.

Your father, she said, and her voice quaked and would
soon crack but then there was a great crack in the air and
the room quaked and the lamp went out and we turned
to the window, my mother and me, and the night sky was
red and my mother turned back to me and I could not see

her face clearly anymore. But her voice changed. It was very calm.

She said, Your father came from far away.

Like the dragon who was the ruler of all the oceans, I said.

She knew this story, too. All Vietnamese know this story. She hesitated and then her hand came out and she cupped me under the chin with her palm. I wanted it to be true just as I had always heard it. But she waited and waited and then she said, This is different. Her hand fell and she looked again at the red sky. There was a dark chattering out there in the distance. Gunfire.

And then she said, This dragon did not live in a kingdom of water. He lived with his father and mother in a distant place and they were all dragons there. And his father went every day into a fiery hole and this was the wealth and the work of his kingdom. Fire. He would descend into fire and there were other dragons there and some of them were his enemies. They were killers. Your father's father once fought a terrible fight deep in this fiery place and he killed his enemy there. He did not know this but he fought his enemy and killed him for the sake of a beautiful little girl, a fairy princess on the far side of the world, for if he had lost this fight and had died there, his own son would never have been born and then this girl child would never have been born either. But he killed the seed of another dragon and his own did not die and so your father was born and he grew from a child into an adult. His mother was gentle and feared for him but when he was old enough he, too, went into the fire. And then one day his father told him that there were places of fire far away and there were new enemies and he must go there and fight them. And he did. And he met me and he loved me and he planted a child in me with his seed, a beautiful child, but before she was born, he died in the midst of fire.

The redness of the sky was very bright now. My mother had rushed to the ending of the story and I was a little bit angry at her. I wanted her to tell this again. Tell it more slowly. She rushed through the places that I wanted to hear about the most, but now she was crying and I had much to think about already and when she bent to me and kissed me and then lay down, I let her hold me close and I said no more.

I never had a chance to ask her about that story again. A few nights later the sounds of the rockets and the gunfire would not stop and there were people running in the streets and everyone knew that the end was near. Or the beginning, as I would later learn. But my mother knew nothing of the future. All she knew was her own guilt and the fear that all she had done would be found out and destroy her and me as well. So on a night that I now know to have been April 29, 1975, she called me to her from my grandmother's place and when I came into our rooms she had a bag packed and sitting by the door. Much of this is not very clear to me in my memory. She was dressed in black pantaloons and a drab green peasant shirt and a woven conical hat sat on top of her case. I must have known what would happen. I felt heavy in my arms and legs, as if I had just woken from a deep sleep. She spoke to me and I heard little. I am sure she told me how much she loved me. I am sure she told me how sad she was to do this. But I remember nothing clearly until she took me by the shoulders and crouched down and brought her face very near mine. She did not smell of the American soap that was so pure. She did not smell at all. There was sweat on her brow. She looked at me with her eyes full of tears, but her mouth was hard.

You must understand this, she said. You must never speak of me again. I am dead. You are an orphan. The people who are coming into our country now are hard people. They would kill me for what I have done. They would make life very bad for you if they knew whose daughter you are. They would take you away and they would hurt you. Do you understand?

I heard the words now, very clearly. But I did not understand. Still, I said yes to my mother. I knew that the world was changing in some terrible way. That was enough to know at this moment. She nodded and she looked away to the window and then her eyes came back to me and some struggle was inside her.

She said, There is one more thing you must know, but in knowing it you must now never speak of it to anyone. Do you understand? This is a most important secret. I have thought of telling you this but I was afraid. Why should you have to carry this secret? But your grandmother thinks it is right. And since you will live with her now instead of me, I must obey her. Will you keep this secret from everyone forever?

Yes, I said. Yes.

Then she told me this thing. Your father is dead, she said. He is dead.

I know, I said.

More, she said. He was an American.

I could not quite take that in for a moment. That was a sea too far away and too deep to think of. And not a sea at all, she had said. A kingdom of fire.

And steam was rising hot in my face. The water was boiling. I took the pot off the hot plate and I waited to let all these things pass from me. Ben was in the other room, I was making tea for him, and he was the only man I wished to understand.

I carried the tea tray in and stood before him and he looked up at me from where he sat cross-legged on the mat and his eyes were dark, like they had been wood burned to charcoal by some great fire. He knew there should be a picture on my altar and in his eyes were questions about me.

I gently placed the tray on the table, covering the white cranes. I crouched there and I poured the tea and I tried not to make a sound, letting the tea slide from the spout softly, one cup and then another, Ben's eyes on me. I looked once at him and did not look again, not even a glance, and then I brought the pot to the tray very slowly, letting it settle there in absolute silence. I heard him breathing. It was very faint, but I was aware of it even then. It felt as if he was touching me. Just hearing his breath was a private thing, a touch like I had never felt before.

The shrine is for my father, I said. He died in the war and there are no pictures. My mother is also dead.

I said no more. Ben's breath sighed out long and soft and it was a deep kiss of sympathy to my ear. I'm sorry, he said.

I did not answer. The tea was poured. I kept my eyes lowered and I did not tell my secret.

Our lips touch. Tien's hand is at the back of my head and she pulls me to her and we kiss. This gesture of desire, the press of her hand on me to bring us to this touch: though I will soon be forty-eight years old, there has not been any moment in my life when I've felt desired in this way. And before I met Tien, my own desire was a ragged thing, a scrap of retread by the highway kicked up now and then by the force of a passing truck.

My first night on this return to Vietnam I wandered out of the hotel and down to the hub of the city, a circular fountain where Le Loi and Nguyen Hue cross, and I stood there in the fine mist from the rush of water and I faced toward the gingerbread City Hall, its facade full of columns and spires and lit up with spotlights and Ho Chi Minh's bronze statue in the square in front, him sitting on a tree stump with his arm around a little girl, and behind me was the river. And all about me the streets were full of the Vietnamese on their motorbikes and they were racing around and around.

And one motorbike went around the circle a second time and a third, probably more times before that until a faint *hey you* slid out of the roar of motors and finally caught my attention and I saw the two faces turned to me. There was a young man with a mustache driving, and sitting behind him, her arms around his waist, was a woman in a short skirt. The second time around, their faces were turned again to me and he smiled and slipped his chin a couple of quick times and she was young, the flash of her was pretty and there was a fine mist of envy prickling at the back of my neck because of her arms around the man, even though I knew what was going on and I could buy that privilege for myself. The third time she blew me a kiss, and her night-dark hair was rolled at the back of her head and she had a long, slender neck and her shoulders were bare and she was beautiful. But she and her pimp did not have time to circle again before the mist was just fountain spray, and I wiped it away and turned from the street, and though it was my first night in Vietnam and though the first woman I ever thought I loved was a Vietnamese woman and though this face circling behind me now and wondering why I had stopped looking at her was a beautiful face, there was nothing running in my limbs hut the heaviness of night and the drag of a dozen time zones.

I went back to my hotel just off what used to be Tu Do Street and I stood at the window for a little while. I would not pluck her from the flow of traffic but I watched the little stretch of Tu Do between the buildings below, and the motorbikes coursed there without cease, like blood, and I raised my eyes to where the river was, visible that afternoon but invisible now in the dark. There was only a great red neon HEINEKEN on what I knew to be the far bank.

And I thought, What kind of man am I? I had traveled a long way and I was tired, but I had not touched a woman for nearly two years and the woman out there was beautiful and though I would have to pay her, that's how it had begun with Kim. Not that I was looking for love that way again. It was about being a man, and I have lived most of my life among men, at the mill, in the Army, out over the road with the big rigs, and no man I ever knew would understand that I couldn't be with that woman who was out there in the dark, ready to come in to me. That I couldn't pay her what she wanted and bring her into this room and lie with her nakedness and her softness and her wetness and find that very good. I didn't fully understand it myself.

I turned from the window and the room was dim but I did not want light. I lay down on the bed and the paddle fan moved above me. I was on top of the covers, clothed, as if I wanted to think, as if I wanted to lie there and not have anything in my head at all. I didn't. And then Mattie lay down next to me.

I closed my eyes and the fan clucked softly overhead and it was quite a few years before Mattie and me could figure out this wasn't the way life was supposed to be. In the dark, though, on my first night back in Saigon, she just lay beside me and it was her from sometime out in the dim middle of our marriage, sometime after there was no more South Vietnam, sometime when everyone who never went there was trying to pretend none of that ever happened, sometime out there when, for me, the things you'd expect to be the toughest had actually finally stopped being a very big deal—the dead men and the wild thrash of fear when there were a lot of bad sounds going on around you and you could look out of all the windows of your truck and you could see just these rice paddies and jagged trees and a road disappearing in smoke and there was no place to run and the thrashing inside you would begin so hard you'd think you'd never be able to draw another breath and that was how you'd die, without a mark on your body, just slumped over dead from the fear, and it tasted like there was blood in your mouth but there was no blood, not yet. But that hard stuff was pretty much gone by the middle of my marriage to Mattie. It was like getting over the death of your father and then getting over the death of your mother. You think it'll never end but then one day you realize that it has pretty much ended. The hard stuff was gone, and the marriage was, too. The passion of my fear was gone. And whatever it was that passed for passion between her and me was gone, too.

I opened my eyes and Mattie had vanished and the fan blades sliced above my body, softly, softly, over and over, and I wanted to think that sex had nothing to do with what had brought me to this bed in this country where I once had desperately counted the days till I could leave and never look back. But there was a fullness in me, something unreleased, and I recognized it as the readiness for sex and it felt connected to something important, and I knew the way it was supposed to be: you go inside a woman and you release the stuff of you that suddenly feels so important and she releases something in herself to you, and from all that, a new thing is supposed to come about, a single thing between the two of you, your two selves, a thing that is whole. That was the alternative to the truck-stop view of sex. And it was something I wanted, something I sensed when I found my mother touching my father's back in the kitchen.

But on that first night of this return to Vietnam I lay on the bed and I knew it had never been that way for me, not with Kim, not with Mattie, not with a few others, and it could never be that way with the woman out there on the back of the motorbike. But I also knew I was in Vietnam because of a desire just like that one you can have about sex, the desire for things to be whole. And I know now how that desire got stuck over here, how it failed to make it onto the plane back home in 1967.

It was out somewhere along Vietnam's Highway One.
I came to the war and I was driving trucks and that was
going to be okay, I was driving in the Saigon area, from
Newport, the place where the supplies came in by ship,
to the dispersion points around the area and it was going
to be okay for me, and I thought the biggest danger I faced
was running over somebody in the goddamn streets of Saigon, where there was just chaos, it seemed to me, where
everybody just swarmed and there was only that. But in
1966 there was a big rush of stuff into the country and lots
of new units and I found myself driving a deuce-and-a-
half in a convoy up Highway One in the direction of Phan
Thiet. It was hot and the cab of the truck was full of the
smell of diesel because I was just a couple of vehicles back
of our lead ACAVs, the armored cavalry assault vehicles,
which had the dirtiest damn engines in the world, waving
thick tails of smoke. I couldn't see what was on the sides
really, a rubber plantation for a ways, I remember, the
thin trunks cut and bleeding latex, and then rice paddies
and a distant tree line, and then red earth, brick kilns
along the way.

Highway One was a long road and I wanted to take it in
and maybe parts of me did, but I mostly had to keep my
eyes on the truck in front of me and the trail of smoke,
and there was always the smell of diesel, a smell it would
take me years to finally connect to other things, to the

smell of oranges and nights on the California coast when
nothing was going to come out of the trees to try to kill
me. And somewhere along the way the day ripped open
with a sound like the air was made of tin and was shear-
ing and then clanging and we stopped dead and there was
a roar of tiny sounds all cluttering together and then a
hard ping off my hood and I was sitting transfixed and
then the truck in front of me scooted sideways and there
was a flare at the front of it and I saw an ACAV hustle
itself to the right, into the scrub off the side of the road.
Now I knew to go down under the steering wheel and
I pressed at my shoulders to turn me and a little puff of
white skittered across my hood and I was pushing hard at
my own body focusing somewhere up around my shoulders trying to go down, go down to a place where I could
not see the glass around me which held a bright flash of
the sun which was somewhere out there watching all this
and the glass also held a dim image of my face, I could
see my own eyes looking at me going down toward the
seat, falling but not very fast at all and this puzzled me
why I was suddenly so slow. And there was another ping
and splash of sound, glass, and I was down on the seat
and I thought I was there of my own free will, not hit, and
my body was cold but there was no pain anywhere and
there wouldn't be, I was okay, and then the ACAVs began
their mad minute—the vast sky-wide cry of cannon and

machine gun—and I knew that the tree line, where the others were, would shred and dissolve now and my head pounded with the sound.

And I saw only one dead body.

No. Not dead. It's odd I should remember him as dead, though he probably died later. But he was alive when I saw him, alive and standing just off the road next to his truck. The fight was over. Suddenly I could hear the shallow little pulse of my own breath, fast now, so fast I was going dark behind my eyes. I dragged myself up and I was sitting and I gripped my steering wheel and tried to slow down inside. A sunburst of cracks was before me in the window and my breath slowed and settled, and then there began a slow beat, like great wings, flapping in my chest, and outside, cut by the cracks, was a deuce-and-a-half angled off the road and the cab was twisted and smoldering and the flapping in me felt like it would lift me up now and I had to deal with this breathing thing one more time and I wanted to open the door and maybe get out but I didn't have the strength right then and so I put my face into the open door window and he was out in the scrub by the road, just a few yards away from his truck. There was no horror to this for me. Not like you'd expect. When I've dreamed of him, the few times I have since 1966, it's been with a sadness that had nothing to do with his body, or even to do with him at all. He was a

young guy, my age at the moment I was looking at him,
twenty or so, a blondish guy I never saw before, though
I think he'd been driving that deuce-and-a-half ahead of
me. He was standing upright there in the scrub dressed
in fatigue pants and a green tee-shirt and his right arm
was gone. Just ripped away somehow and he was looking
down at the place where it had been a few moments ago
and he had this knot in his brow. He wasn't making a
sound and he was standing there by the road as if everything was okay but he just suddenly realized, with a kind
of serious puzzlement, that he wasn't all there. That's
what the dream has been, the few times I've dreamed of
him. He's looking at himself with that quizzical expres-
sion and I look down at my own body and I find one arm
and then the other and I have both my legs and though I
think I can be sure that I have every part of my body, I
know I'm not complete.

I try not to think of my father at that moment when Ben's
lips first touch mine. But the smell of the incense of my
father's shrine is very clear to me and I try to hold that
smell away from me and it is very hard. I have lit the slender tips of the incense a thousand times for him, more,
five thousand times perhaps—every night since I was ten

years old—and it is not easy to pretend that this smell is not here, that his soul is not here, but I want only to feel the touch of Ben's lips. And little claws of panic are burrowing deep into me in the place between my breasts where his hand touched me moments ago. I think: I am missing my first kiss with Ben. I concentrate on the soft touch of his mouth. I press my mouth harder against him and his lips open mine slightly and he is touching the inside of my lip with his tongue and I am forgetting now, forgetting the past, I am touching Ben and I am not expecting what is next. I feel suddenly his hand on my bare stomach and then it slides down and inside my pantaloons and I yield to him as easily as the silk and his hand goes to that place between my legs.

There are many things that I do not fully understand about my body. I know the ways of understanding from before the revolution: a woman's body was given to a man by her parents and it was to make children for him. I know the ways of my mother: a woman's body was something of such little value to her that it could be sold to any man. But the ways of our leaders now are not very clear. We are to be modest about our bodies because they are to be given to the service of the state. I think in order to make children for our country. Something like that. There were words about these things at first when the country was finally made one. That was in those early years when

the streets of Saigon were thick at night with darkness
except for a few scraps of fire in a gutter, a kerosene lamp
burning down an alleyway. And there was such a terrible
quiet. I sometimes wish in this era of our country that the
motorbikes would stop outside in the streets, but they are
better than the silence. I can wake at three or four in the
early mornings now and it is quiet but it is quiet from a
sound that was there only a few hours ago and will come
again soon, it is still not like those years when the sun
went down and there was no electric light and there was
the smell of wood fire and a little kerosene and there was
no gasoline and there was only the faint click of bicycle
chains and we all whispered to each other. In those years
I think a woman's body was intended to make children
for our great socialist state, but now I do not know. The
lights returned and the sounds, but I do not know where
our bodies are.

When I met Ben, before he touched me for the first
time, I crouched in my bathroom one night and I sponged
my naked body and I began to tremble. It must have been
because of him. He had been in the other room that very
day and I had served him tea and now he was gone, but
something of him remained, like a faint scent of smoke,
and I was naked and this part that he would soon touch felt
as if it had begun to pout, like a child, pout from being left
out of something she wanted very much to do. I stood up

and I was still wet from my bath and I was naked. I moved to the little mirror and I could see only my face and my throat and only a little of my chest, not my breasts at all. I was modest still, in this great socialist state, modest even to myself in my own bathroom.

The mirror hung with a cord from a nail and I touched it with my fingertip just at the bottom and it moved and my face disappeared and my breath caught when I saw my own nipples like this, before me, apart from me, and it was because of him. I tipped the mirror farther and I could see the little dark flame of hair coming up from that secret place between my legs and I let the mirror go and my face rushed back and quaked there and I remembered my grandmother's question, and though I saw only me in the mirror, I did not feel alone: I had seen my nipples, my secret place, as he would someday see them, naked before him. And here was my face as he would see it. I tried to smile for him, but the pouting between my legs was very strong, and I had to stop because it was becoming painful now, this pleasure, this yearning.

I dried myself and I covered myself with a silk robe and I lay down on my bed. And I thought that if I ever had a baby I would wish to have a girl, though my husband would certainly want a boy. If my husband were a Vietnamese. I blushed at this. This thought carried the possibility that I would not marry a Vietnamese and I knew who I meant. I wondered if American men wanted only boys or if they could love a girl child too. I would raise her as a good daughter of a great socialist state but I would do the old ways, as well.

In Vietnam we worry about a child, if it will live very long. My grandmother told me how in the countryside, for the first month, the mother would remain in bed with her baby and the baby was wrapped tight in its bedclothes. The baby would be held safe from the sun and the rain and the winds and from those in the spirit world who would take her away with them. Then at one month old the baby would be brought into the sunlight and everyone in the village would gather around and they would take a white jasmine flower made wet from special water from the altar in the pagoda and they would hold the flower over the baby and a drop of the water would fall into the baby's mouth. This would make the baby's words sweet as the scent of jasmine all her life.

I asked my grandmother if that was done for me and she shook her head sadly and she said, "No, I tell you this thing because as you become a woman of Vietnam you should know this for your own child someday."

I was sad when she said this. I wished to speak with words sweet as jasmine, but I could not. Perhaps I should not be sad about this, in this modern Vietnam, working in the job that I do. Perhaps I am better off this way. But

I would want this thing for my own daughter. I lay on the bed on the night I saw my body through Ben's eyes in my mirror and I dreamed of my own child, and this was so foolish, I realized. I did not know this man, this man I was already thinking of marrying. But that has always been the way of my country. In the old customs, the parents made the choice for their child and the woman met her husband only after they were betrothed. Is that so very different from this? I sat with Ben and I made tea for him and he knew about the spirits of the ancestors and he spoke gently to me and I loved his face with its dark eyes and dragon's jaw. So I thought of how I would let a drop of water fall on my daughter's lips.

Though the memory that had come upon me did not stop. I asked one more question of my grandmother when she taught me this necessary thing about being a Vietnamese mother. I asked, "Did you do this for my mother?"

She seemed a little surprised at this question, though she should not have been. "Yes," she said.

I was thirteen or fourteen years old at that time and my mother had been gone for a while and I was glad she was safe and I wished she was dead and I was happy she had the drop of jasmine water on her lips when she was a baby and I was angry she did not give me this precious thing. And then I thought of something that made me question it all. It was this woman, my mother, who had received the precious water. "So it must not work," I said. My mother had spoken some sweet words, I suppose, but none that I could remember, and certainly not all of her words for her whole life, and even if her words to all the men had sounded sweet to them, surely that was not the point of this tradition, to sweeten the words of a prostitute for the men who would buy her body.

Still, as I lay on my bed, with Ben just behind all of my thoughts, I decided that when the time came, I would go to a pagoda and put the precious water on a jasmine flower and let it fall from there onto the mouth of my child. She would have this thing that I never had. And she would have a mother who was not forced to flee and never return. And she would have a father.

A father. I lay on my bed and my body felt things it had never felt and I dreamed of a child, and who was the father in this dream? An American. Did I imagine he would stay in Vietnam and we would live in this room where I grew up? Did I imagine I would leave Vietnam and go to America? No. I did not imagine anything except a child in my arms and Ben nearby. All the rest did not exist. I did not even think of Ben touching me. Not directly. My body dreamed of that in its own way, quaking and swelling and trembling, but in my head was only a jasmine flower and a drop of water and a child and she was

beautiful and her eyes moved to mine and I could see myself there, as in tiny dark mirrors, and then I felt another
thing in my body, a flexing, a fierceness, and I wanted
things for her and in that wanting I grew angry. I thought,
Was it really for me that my mother stayed away? Things
are different now in Vietnam. She could come to Ho Chi
Minh City and she could come to the very street where
she lived and she could find me in the very place where
her own mother once lived and no one would harm her.
The government does not care about that now. They do
not care about the whores of the Americans. Is it really
for my sake that she has never returned? Or is it for her
own? Did she grow tired of her child?

Or is she dead. Did she die for my sake. She was right
to keep my American self hidden. The children who
were clearly the sons and daughters of Americans were
difficult for us all to understand after the nation was
made one.

But that was because the hearts of these children were
still American. They still wanted the things of that country. My government believed this and they sent those
children to America, where they might be happy. I was
never like those others. I could keep my American self
hidden because it never really existed. It died with my
father even before I was born. I had no father. There
was never a father. His blood was spilled before I was

born and it spilled from me as well, even in my mother's womb. His blood was gone. But did my mother's blood fill me in its place? Or am I a cup half full?

I thought these things on my bed on the day Ben was first here and I opened my robe and I was naked and I looked to the mat where he drank tea and I had filled his cup many times and he drank and my own cup sat before me full and growing cold. I did not think of myself. I was very happy sitting there and filling his cup and watching him drink what I had brought him. And my body in its nakedness yearned now and I understood that yearning and I knew I wanted him to touch me, as if I was the luckiest of arranged brides in the whole history of Vietnam, as if my mother and my father had chosen for me a most beautiful man and he and I had come together on our wedding night as strangers, really, as is our custom, but we loved each other instantly and we touched each other and it was very beautiful and we thanked our parents for arranging this. But the more my body yearned for him as I lay there, the more I understood all that had gone before. Yes, I was a cup only half full. Yes, my father's blood was gone and nothing had filled me in those empty places. But with this man I felt it was possible. I did not care that he was American. I held my child and the drop of jasmine water fell on her lips and she spoke his name. Ben.

She says, "Ben." When I put my hand on that place between Tien's legs, she speaks my name and I think, This is the moment it will all stop. I've gone too fast. And I stop and I'm ready to move my hand away and I'm beginning to curse myself inside because I don't want this to end and I've fucked it up now. Fucked up the most important thing of all, for even that brief touch is different from anything I've ever felt and it is suddenly very important. All up and down the forefinger edge of my left hand is her softness and I'm stunned by that, it's her, it's Tien I touch, and I touch her in a place that seems so entirely part of her and so entirely secret that I am drawn out of myself and it feels as if I've just discovered my hand, I've never had a real feeling there before, but now I do, and I rise to her and I know that I will soon find other parts of me that I never knew I had, never did have. I raise my hand from her and it's flushed and I feel my heart beating there and Tien says something to me in Vietnamese. It's urgent, but it's soft. Then I think she realizes how she has spoken and she repeats it in English. "I didn't mean for you to stop."

"You said my name. I didn't know."

"I said your name because I was happy you touched me there."

"Are you sure?" I ask.

"I told you before that it is all right."

"About your breasts. I didn't know if it applied . . ."

"It does."

"I'm hearing myself now," I say. "I sound like a damn fool."

"You sound very nice."

"It feels like the first time for me, too."

Her voice grows eager. "Does it really feel like that?"

"Yes."

"Though you have done this many times?"

"Not so very many. I don't remember."

And this is true. I can't remember. I have no past, either, it seems. My hand returns to that place and she opens her legs and I have trouble drawing a breath because of the gentleness of her there and because of all that has gone before, as blurred and sometimes blank as my memory is, I have a sharp sense now of the long road to this touching, this sweet and momentous touching.

Earlier she went into her bathroom, as she did the first time I was here. She closed the door and I could not sit down. I did not know I would touch her on this night and I was in a free fall inside, I was white knuckled on whatever it is that I hold inside me in order to steer, and it felt like I'd just gone over a cliff edge and I was falling. And I found myself in front of her ancestor shrine. Half a dozen sticks of incense were stuck in a glass bowl full of white sand. I plucked out one of them, not really with anything in mind. My hands were restless and I plucked one stick of incense and then another and I pulled them all out and held them together and they were cold, the tips were black and cold, the smoke for Tien's father long ago dissolved into the air, and I realized that my hand was trembling. Then I jumped at some sound from the bathroom and I knew I shouldn't be intruding here. I stuck the incense into the sand and I backed away. Water began to run on the other side of her bathroom door. I stood in the center of her room and I looked back to the faceless shrine.

Here was a little monument to family history, which these Vietnamese believe in deeply. So why shouldn't I think at that moment of my own family? Even of things that might, at first glance, seem far from what was about to happen between Tien and me. A little bit of family history that stuck with me and never went away, no matter how many miles of highway I raced over on how many days and nights in the thirty years to come. Tien said her father had died in the war. I thought of my own father, who never had a chance to die in a war and I thought of how that disappointed him. He was in his mid-thirties when the Second World War began and he was working in steel, a crucial industry, and they wouldn't take him. He had a bad knee, too, though not bad enough that he couldn't work the labor gang, and he was as strong as two men, and he told this to the draft board more than a few times, but they still wouldn't take him. And if he had gone to war and he had died there, I would never have been born. He realized that. He even told me once.

It was the summer of 1965 and he'd got me a job at the mill the year before, right after I graduated from high school with not much in my head to do with my life. My mother wanted me to go to college real bad. She taught me to like books and I did, but she had come to love them, and it took something like love to want to actually study them and I think I loved my father and he loved the mill and he loved working there, so I did what he wanted of me. He was a foreman at the North Plant by then and he got me on at the blast furnace operation doing what he did for a large part of his life, working the labor gang.

It was sometime in July that year when we met one afternoon before we were due on our night shifts at four. It was at a bar just down the road from the blast furnace and the Cards were on the radio, playing the Cubs in Wrigley Field and Bob Gibson was pitching. I remember that because it made the silence between my father and me comfortable, baseball did. I was only nineteen but if you had steel toes on and goggles around your neck and you smelled like the mill already even though you were still sweating clean, before a shift, they didn't ask any questions at the Half Moon Bar, so my father and I were nursing a couple of

Buds, neither of us being real drinkers, and Harry Caray was pissed on the radio about some sloppy Cardinal play in the field and that morning's *Globe Democrat* was lying faceup on the bar with a headline about the Marines in Da Nang, and it turned out this was what my father was thinking about in his silence.

Finally he said, "You think you ought to go?"

"Where?"

"To Vietnam. To the war."

"I wasn't thinking about it," I said.

"I missed out."

"I know." I knew that whole story already, had known it for some time.

"If this thing gets bigger, they'll need men," he said.

I nodded at this and I turned the bottle in my hands a few times and the label was going soggy and I started peeling it away and what was going on in me was the way he said "men" and a feeling I'd had for as long as I could remember was starting up again, a feeling that had put me in that bar at that moment with steel-toed shoes on and goggles around my neck, and that was the feeling that my father thought of me as a man and he knew I could do the tough things, no question about it, and I stripped the label off the bottle and wadded it up to a dense little ball and put it down gently. It was already decided, I realized. I was going to end up in that war. I was going to do this thing for the reason I'd done about everything else up to that moment. For him. All but reading a bunch of books and trying to figure out how to control my words in certain circumstances, and that I'd done for my mother.

"I could handle that," I said.

"I know you could," he said, and his voice surprised me in how soft it had gone. We neither of us had looked at each other since we sat down there, shoulder to shoulder at the bar. I wanted to look at him now, but I didn't.

He said, "Sometimes I make it sound like all I got is regrets about not fighting the war. But it was okay. If I'd gone I might not've come back so I could have a son."

He said that to me. This man didn't have a lot of words, usually. And maybe after him suggesting I should go to war and put my life on the line in a way he'd missed, maybe then he had to try to tell me it wasn't because he didn't value that life of mine. How could this man who was my father say such a thing? Maybe that was the way. I stood before Tien's shrine and I turned my face away from this thing that wouldn't even let a man die and be done with it. I didn't want my eyes to be full of fucking tears when she came in wearing her silks and still damp from her washing.

But the memory wouldn't let go of me. That was the time he told me about when they tried to kill him at the mill. My father had a long life before I came along. He was at the mill in the Depression, and the summer before Roosevelt won for the first time, there was a lot of bad stuff going down. My father hated the guy who owned the mill and what he was doing to the workers. So he got mixed up with the radicals. He didn't know anything about communism. He just wanted things to be better for the men who worked the furnaces with him.

When my father said he was glad he had a son, I did turn to him. He was watching his beer. I waited for him to look my way, though it was enough he'd spoken the words. He'd been planning this for a while, I think. He had to do it the way he'd figured it out. He kept his eyes on his beer, or maybe on his hands, his great, thick hands lying there on the bar before him.

And then he told me a story about himself. He said, "In '32, things were bad in this town. The men who work this place had enemies they couldn't even figure out. But I was trying to. The biggest of the enemies was the owner of Wabash Steel. John J. Hagemeyer. I never made a secret of my feelings. So he sent one of his goons into the B-furnace stove with me. In those days we'd have two-men teams that went into the stove for short times to poke out the clogs of flue dust in the brickwork. We couldn't be in there for long. It was the toughest work on the labor gang. Nothing like it. We'd go up the furnace and then into a trap at the top with nothing but a teapot lamp and a steel rod and we'd go down into the stove and it was like climbing down into the fire. But once, Hage-meyer sent one of his boys in with me and there was a place in there on one side that was an open shaft straight down to the combustion chamber. I was working near there and the goon jumped me, tried to throw me down. But I fought him a short, hard fight and it was him who went down the shaft and died. Just the thirty seconds or so of fight almost killed me in that place too. There was no way to breathe. But I dragged myself back out of there and your mama and I eventually got away to the west for a time. Till the war came and all my enemies at Wabash Steel were either gone or dead. Even Hagemeyer. By 1941 he was just a street name. So we come back."

It was the longest he'd ever spoken to me, I think. I was breathless from hearing his voice for all of these words, wondering when they would stop, grateful for them no matter what it was he was saying. He almost died. Fourteen years before I was born. Fighting a man. Killing a man. These were things a father might tell a son someday, but why on this day? It wasn't until later that I wondered why, and of course I never asked him. Maybe it was because he had just told his only child that he should go to war. Maybe he wanted me to know that he had faced death himself in what he saw as another kind of war. Without that, he felt he had no right to ask me.

Maybe it came up because of it being another chance for me never to have been born. He was glad I was born and he was determined to tell me and that could have been the connection in his head. And maybe all of it, all of it, including why I should go to Vietnam, had something to do with deciding what it is you're ready to die for.

Whatever the reasons, he just said the things he wanted to say and he didn't say any more and I didn't ask. I turned my face to my own beer and I laid my hands on the bar and there was a blur of baseball words around us and the whoosh of a semi rushing past outside and I drag my wrist across my forehead, wiping away the sweat here in Tien's apartment, and there is no longer a threat of tears. The past is no longer a matter of tears and smoke. It's simple now. I went away. I came back. He died. My mother died.

And this memory that came to me before Tien was about to emerge from her bath, I see now that the talk with my father was the first marker on a long road that would one day bring me to her bed. And the switchback that would have prevented it was there, too. If it had been my father who had gone down that shaft. But in those thirty seconds in the stove at B-furnace more than sixty years ago and half a world away, my father killed a man, and as a result, Tien came out of her bathroom with her hair and throat and hands still damp and she found me there, and now I have put my hand in that soft and secret place on her body and she speaks my name and I am afraid I have gone too fast but she says it's okay and I move my hand once more to that place and touch her.

This time, knowing for certain that it's okay, knowing that Tien and I will make love, I flare inside, I have climbed down inside the stove and the brickwork is clean and the heat seethes through and I burn. Sweetly, but I burn. I am hot in my clothes and blocked in some painful way and her dark eyes are watching me, waiting, and I bend to her and our lips touch again, and very gently I move my hand upon her and she sighs into our kiss, I feel her breath move into me as if I've been dragged dying from the sea and she wants to bring me back to life.

And still I'm hesitant. I must ask her first. I pull my mouth away from hers and say, "Can I take these clothes off?"

"Yours or mine?" she says.

"Both. Though I meant mine."

"Am I ready?"

I hear how childish I sound. I should know if my own body is ready to take a man into it. It has done this thing before. No. I have spoken a true lie to Ben and I must hear its truth for myself. It is not just a matter of readiness for a man. It is this *one* man. No one else has been Ben.

"Are you ready?" he repeats, completely baffled by the question, and I am embarrassed.

"Yes, I am," I say, pretending that it is his question and I am giving him my answer. This confuses him some more. "Thank you for asking me," I add.

He stares at me, trying to figure all this out.

"Yes you can," I say, trying to move on to the question of our clothes.

"Are you doing this on purpose?" he asks. His voice is gentle and in the neon light I can see his brow knit and his mouth shape a smile. He is enjoying me.

"Yes. I am a great kidder," I say, though if it is true about me, then it has come about only in the past few moments.

"I'm very confused now," he says, but there is a playful thing in his voice and there is nothing confusing about what is going on between his hand and that special place on my body. I know this for sure.

I say, "I will help make things clear for you. Yes I am ready. Yes you can remove these clothes. Yours and mine."

He smiles again and he brings his face close and he kisses me on the lips and I like that kiss, but as soon as it is over, I say, "I am not kidding." Because I am ready.

He nods and he says, "Thank you."

"No, thank you," I say.

And he begins with me. He pulls back and I am already naked above the waist and I am very comfortable with that and he puts his hands on the rim of my pantaloons. And I expect things to be floating by in my head, like the bits of the jungle in the Saigon River, I expect the things I always live with in my head to just keep on passing through: my mother and my father and my grandmother and my work and the Socialist Republic of Vietnam—what it is and what it expects of me—and even the dragons and the jasmine flowers of our lovely stories. But when Ben puts his hands inside the top edge of my pants and his knuckles lie warm on my hips, all those things vanish from me and there is only' the slip of his hands over my hipbones and down the outer edges of my thighs and past my knees and my calves and my ankles, and as his hands move I feel my nakedness emerging for him in their wake, and then the silk bunches over my feet and then is gone and I close my eyes and all that I am is in my skin, all that I need ever to know opens with my pores into the moist air of this room and I wait with my eyes closed, not because I am afraid but

because in this moment I have become my skin and seeing has nothing to do with that, and then Ben's skin falls
upon me, his thigh against my thigh, his chest against my
chest, I open my eyes and his face is to my side and I turn
to him. We touch our lips. He touches my cheek with his
lips. I close my eyes again and his lips are on my eyelids,
and now there is a new place of touching. A clear, hard
spot on my hip and I know what part of him is doing this,
and then he shifts and the spot disappears and he is over
me and I wait. I close my eyes and I feel as if I am waiting
beneath a jasmine flower, waiting for a drop to fall on my
mouth so that I can speak for the first time. And then in
that special place on my body, that place of such strange
and sometimes sloppy mystery, that place that sometimes
I love and sometimes I shun, Ben is beginning to nudge
his way in, and I wait for this now, I wait for the rest of
my life to begin, and I open a little and a little more and
then there is a hard, fleshy wrenching, a bloom of pain
that unfolds quick and sharp into my womb and my thighs
and I gasp.

"I'm sorry," he says.

"I'm sorry," I say. I do not want him to stop. I open my
eyes to Ben. His brow is knit above me. He is not moving.
I feel held open. And the pain is blunt now. And then it is
tiny. And then it is gone.

"Do you want me to stop?" he asks.

"Go forward for the good of the revolution," I say and this surprises me. It is from some schoolbook from the early days of the liberation. Perhaps I am a great kidder after all. We both laugh and that special part of me clenches with the laughter and his special part moves a little, and the effect, I quickly decide, is very nice and I would like to have that effect with no laughter. "No more questions now," I say.

And now he makes love to me. And I am close to him. I am close to this man. I suddenly understand how far away people are from each other, even passing near in the street, even brushing shoulders, even looking into each other's eyes and speaking each other's names, there is this great empty space between us and now there is no space at all, I clutch Ben's naked back and he is inside me and my body is a blur, the very cells of it are twisted away from each other and perhaps they have always been like that and I am just realizing it and I gather for Ben, everything is twisted apart so that something can find its way out and gather in me, ready for him, and now suddenly all of this, all these cells of mine, rush into focus, I am pulsing hard where our bodies are joined and everything is suddenly very clear and I am put together again.

And he is still moving and I realize that he has not yet given to me and he says, "I will come out of you now." I

know what he means and for him to spill himself outside
of me seems a terrible thing. I feel him drawing out.

"No," I say and I hold him tight. "And do not ask if I am
sure."

He slides back inside me and I am happy for that.

And on this night of the first time I make love to this
man, I hold Benjamin Cole close to me. And we are naked.
And we are sweating. And then I know he has given to me.
And I am a cup filled to overflowing.

She does not want me outside her body and I don't question her. What's between us seems to call for this. She
knows it and I know it. But still there is a moment just
before I am about to run inside her that I think it will be
like it always has been, this thing will have its own life
and I am clenched tight down there, it is near to time,
and I'm waiting for something to snap free, some hitch
that will lose a pin and my body will rush on and I'll be
left behind in the center of an empty highway wondering
where I went.

But I can hear her breathing. Short, quick, soft in my
ear, and she clings to me hard and our bodies are slick
and I can't sort out one part from another, there's no
single place where there's a pin to slip and we'll break

apart, not even where I grow leaden with readiness, not even that hard dangling place is separate now, we are fused together, all up and down us, from the stroke of her breath on my face to the press of her insteps on my thighs we are one body with parts long lost, missed only in our dreams, rejoined, and I rush now and she shapes a sound and it moves through me and we open our mouths together and cry out and we press tighter and my face is in her hair and her hair is dark and the darkness smells faintly of soap and of incense and it smells, too, of diesel and of oranges and though I can see nothing of my body I know from the clutch of her and the smell of her that I am complete.

And we do not separate our bodies for a long while. At some moment we turn onto our sides, still joined, a world spinning on its axis, but we neither of us want to let go after what we've done, and we lie without speaking, and whenever she makes some slight movement, the shift of a leg, the slide of an arm, the tiniest adjustment of her face against my chest, it surprises me a little and then it delights me, she is someone other than me but she is me as well, I feel the movement of her body as my own movement and I am not only whole, I am multiplied, I am rich with limbs and flesh and voices.

"I love you," I say. I do not expect to say it, though I mean it, and I wait for my other voice to reply.

He says the words that I realize I would myself have said in just a few moments. I pull my face back so I can look at him. His cheek is red from the neon and though his eyes are in shadow, I can see how steady they hold on me. It is very easy to find an answer for him, but I have to struggle to undo a great, hard knot in my throat in order to let my voice through. I say, "I love you."

"Is that true?" he says.

"It is true."

"Are you sure?"

"One of us had to say it first."

"I didn't expect to say it," he says.

"Did you not realize?"

"Not till I said the words."

"I am glad you said it first. Is that selfish of me?"

"No."

"I knew my own feeling for certain, and since you spoke first, I could be certain of yours."

He straightens his face before mine and his eyes are very dark. "You can be certain," he says.

"You can be certain, too," I say. "Of me. This is why you asked is it true. You spoke it first."

"I didn't really doubt you. I think I asked you if it was true to make you say it a few more times."

"I can do that," I say.

"Okay," he says.

"I love you," I say. "I love you."

"Is that selfish of me?"

"No. I am happy to say it. I say it only three times in my life to a man."

I could sense him counting.

"The answer is three," I say.

"Just now?"

"Yes. You are the only one."

His eyes slide away from me and his head angles into the shadow.

"Is there anything wrong?" I ask.

"No," he says, though I know there is something.

I say, "I understand that there were others for you."

He nods at this, though I feel there is still more.

I grow a little afraid. "Is there someone now?"

"No." He says this quickly, a hard little rock of a word, and I believe him.

"I feel something troubling you."

"I don't know," he says. "It's funny. The only thing I can think of that's like this feeling is when I was on the plane that would take me away from Vietnam. You believe you're going to die at any moment and you've believed it so long and so hard that it seems like you've always believed it. Then suddenly you know you're going to live. That's what I'm feeling right now."

I draw him to me and hold him and he holds me. We do this for a while. Then he pulls a little bit away, so he can look into my face.

He says, "It's been two years since I've touched a woman. The touching had all become so bad that I was certain I'd die from it. But I got a test and I'm okay. You can know that. I have nothing in me that will kill us from making love."

I kiss him briefly on the lips and I say, "If you were not sure, you would not have done this thing. I know that."

"How could you know that?" He asks this not like I am a foolish person. I think he wants to understand how it is that I can know to love him.

I say, "I looked into your eyes and I saw all the gentleness I had dreamed for."

"You know so little of me."

"I could say the same thing."

"Ask me," he says. "If there's anything that might frighten you about me. Anything you want to know about me. Ask." And he sits up to show me he is serious.

I sit up, too, and face him. "You are free to love me?"

"Yes. You asked that before."

"Have you been married?"

"Yes."

"Is she dead?" I ask, and my face grows hot from the shame of the question. I wish for it to be so.

"I don't think so. I haven't heard anything about her for some years."

"Did you love her very much?"

"No. Not very much. As much as I could at the time, I guess. It was my fault. As much as I could wasn't very much, is all. I came here, to Vietnam, and then I went home and I'd watched her when I was in high school. She was . . . I don't know. There was something pretty about her, but not soft. That was a kind of thing that I wanted then. I'd watched her in high school and she'd watched me and I guess she saw something in me she liked, but we never got together. Then when I got back from Vietnam, she was working in a dime store and I was living with my parents and when we watched each other again, we could imagine life being better, more interesting, if we lived in some little place together. That was all. And it was better for a time. Better than the heavy days. The way the days just went on, back then. I don't know if this means anything to you, what I'm saying."

It means something to me, I think, when Ben says all of this. I think I know about heavy days. I think it is the same for me, when I am not thinking about what I owe to the country or to the ghost of my father or to the people who come to Vietnam to understand it and I speak to them in English about what we are. In the other times, the days I do not work and my prayers are done, there is some heavy thing in the center of me. I can sit in this very room and I listen to the sound of the motorbikes going by and going by and when there is a little bit of quiet from them, there is a place in the roof of this building that catches the wind and hums a low hum and it just goes on and on and the day is very hot sometimes and I want to sweat but I cannot, my skin fills with my sweat and does not let it go, and this is all there is to my life, just these little sounds and my sweat held in and I grow sad in some dull way. I think this is what Ben is talking about. I have this feeling, too. He and I are the same. But I do not say any of this to him on this night of our first touching. There is something else that trails into my head with his wife, like the smell of her perfume. I say, "Did you have children?"

"We were together more than ten years. But we never had a child."

"Can you have a child?"

"I don't know the answer to that. Mattie and I never checked to see what was the matter. It might've been me. It might've been her. It might've been we just didn't try hard enough. We never did *try,* exactly."

We are sitting before each other on my narrow bed. Our legs are crossed and we are still naked and a feeling comes into me that I never have before. I feel that place between my legs as an opening into me, a way in. But without him inside, I sense the break of me there, and there is the flow of him, cold now, from inside me, and I close my eyes for a moment and there is a spinning in my head. His hands are on my shoulders.

"Are you all right?" he asks.

I open my eyes and things steady. "I am okay now," I say.

He takes his hands away and we are facing each other and I have not looked at him yet. I have not seen that special part of his body. I can cast my eyes down now, I know, and I will see, but as I think to do that, I feel the spinning begin inside again. I will wait to see him there. I will wait. It is enough for now that I can feel my own body in this new way. And there are many things I still want to know.

"How did you decide it was time to stop your marriage?" I ask.

"After I got married, I worked in the steel mill for a while. My father wanted that very badly, me to be back at the mill. So I did that. I got married to Mattie and we rented a little brick house and I took the job my father wanted for me. And nothing felt right. Ever."

"Did the crimes of the war bother you?"

He looks away and I suddenly hear myself. These are true things maybe, that I was taught, but I cannot hear my own voice when I speak them, and if I am sitting naked on a bed with a man and he can look down to see this part of me that is open now, then I want to speak only in my voice. I put my hands on his shoulders, just as he did when I was dizzy. I say, "I do not think you commit any crimes. That was not the way I mean to say it."

He looks back at me and he smiles a little bit, but out of only one side of his mouth. I try to understand what that smile means. I say, "Whatever you did, it was your country that was the criminal." I stop. I hear myself again. I say, "These words come out of my mouth. I do not know where they are from."

He touches my cheek with his fingertips. "It's okay," he says.

"I do know where they are from. I have heard these things all of my life. You hear something all of your life and it makes you talk in a certain way. Even if you have just made love." I turn my face and kiss his fingertips.

When Tien goes into a little riff about the propaganda-talk that's coming out of her mouth, I touch her cheek and she kisses my fingertips and I know I'm loving her more in that moment because of her self-consciousness, and my being here suddenly feels like a thing that began a long time ago without my even knowing it, like this was all set up somehow, and it's an odd feeling, I guess, especially for me to have, because I've never bought into all that, but I can't shake it, this feeling. It's like somebody's arranged this, and I think of my mother.

It was summer and it was late in the afternoon and my father had just disappeared down the street with his lunch box, gone till midnight. I sat on the top step of our front porch and I'd just watched him, the slow roll of his shoulders in his walk, until I couldn't see him anymore. Then there was a rustle behind me and my mother sat down at my side. "He's gone," I said.

She looked off in the direction of the mill and then she turned back to me and she said, "That's okay. I have something for you, anyway."

Suddenly there was a book in her lap. Something from the library that she'd waited till my father was gone to show me. And I can't think of what book it was. I'm sorry, Mama, but I can't think of any of the books, really, though I did read them for you and maybe I got some good from them. But she had a book and then she heard herself, how she'd just sounded. "I don't mean it's okay your father is gone. He likes books too."

I didn't say anything in answer to this. And my mama never wanted to tell me lies. She was very careful about that. So she had to keep talking till things were straight.

She said, "He doesn't *like* them, exactly. But he doesn't have anything against them. He just doesn't love them like you and I do. Like I don't love all the things to do with the mill. You and he love that together. See how many wonderful things there are about you? There's so much more to you than anybody."

She went on like that, listening very carefully to every word she said, trying to correct this or that, down to the tiniest possible misimpression. She comes back to me like that, my mama, when Tien scrambles around trying to undo her words. And I don't think I'm remembering my mother's words from forty years ago. Not really. Not so exactly. But she comes into my head while Tien and me are sitting naked on the bed and we've just made love and Tien is going on in that suddenly familiar way. And I can hear my mother's voice speaking those exact words that may not be exact at all. And she seems tangled up in all of this, somehow, maybe like she was pointing me toward the woman I would someday love.

But I say only, "You remind me of someone."

"Who's that?" Tien says.

"My mother, for a moment."

"Is that good?"

"Yes. It's very good."

"It's gone, though? That feeling is gone?"

"Yes."

"Forgive me, but I'm glad. I like to be your lover better than a mother."

I laugh and put my hand on the calf of her leg. "I do too. It was never anything like that."

"Good."

"And your mother?"

"You don't remind me of her at all."

"Good," I say. "I like being your lover better than a mother."

"I do too."

I love Tien's play, but I'm interested now in a real answer. I say, "Where is your mother?"

"She's dead." Tien says this instantly, looking me straight in the face.

I think of Tien's shrine. "You don't pray for her?"

"She's not worth praying for."

I say this lie to Ben without thinking. It is very easy and that scares me.

Then I speak a hard truth without thinking and maybe that scares me, too, because it is a true thing that I am not ready to say.

"I'm sorry," he says.

So because I say one lie that I do not want to say, I tell him a truth I do not want to say either. "There is no reason to be sorry," I say. "She was a prostitute."

"After your father died?"

He is wanting to make excuses for her. He is asking things that make me want to lie some more. But I also feel I have to speak the truth to this man. I am sitting here naked for him. I have opened my body for him. I do not want all the lies. The lies my mother figured out for me. But to open my mouth and tell all the truth, all at once, seems a terrible thing. I have no strength for that. I try to shape the true words in my head and move them through my voice into this space between Ben and me and I feel suddenly like I am made of stone, like I have looked now at the woman with snakes for hair and all of my insides are turning to stone. But I do manage to say, "No. Before he died."

I hear my voice and I sound very sad. And Ben, being gentle in his way, says no more. He lowers his eyes and murmurs some quiet thing, something full of sorrow and love for me. I love him even more now. Just in these few moments I love Ben more. It fills me with the urge to speak, to have only the full truth about this between us, but it also fills me with the fear of losing him. I say nothing for a while. He says nothing for a while.

Then he speaks. "I don't know who were the crimi-
nals and who were the victims and even what the crime
was, exactly. But I did see some very bad things when I
was here. It's funny. Those things bothered me for a few
months when I first got home. But that faded away. It was
very bad, but I was able to handle that. It wasn't burning
in me after those few months."

"That is a good thing," I say, trying to make up for my
foolish words from before. "I am glad for that."

"But something else took over. It was odd. It was
another feeling and it didn't burn hot but somehow burning dull made it even worse, and it never stopped. Never
did. And it came from me being in the war. I knew that
clearly. Because I was in the war, when I got home and
faced the rest of my life, everything seemed flat, heavy.
There wasn't anything important around me. For a year,
here in Vietnam, I woke up every day and I was scared
and I could see people dying, or walking around and
about to die, not even realizing what was next, though
it was like it was all arranged somehow, because tomorrow's death roster was going to be what it was going to
be, and it could be me who was chosen, and I never lost
a sense of that. And it made everything else . . . I don't
know. Clear, I guess. Strong. I felt alive when I was here.
Keyed up. Back in the States I didn't even know what

being alive felt like sometimes. I'd wake up in the morning and I'd look around at the furniture and out at a few trees in the yard and I'd look at the smoke from the mill in the sky and nothing felt like it was really there. I felt like nobody could kill me now but it didn't mean a fucking thing."

He says all these things and I think I understand him. I put my hand on his leg. He puts his hand on mine and he looks at our hands together. I look down, too. I say, "You tell me things that sound true."

"I haven't said these things before. Except to myself out over the road. I left the mill a few years before Mattie and me broke up and I started driving trucks. I drove a truck in Vietnam and it seemed a good thing to do at home. It got me away from the furniture. But it didn't really solve anything."

He squeezes my hand and lets it go and for a moment his hand and mine lie beside each other. "Look," he says.

But I am already determined to say something. "My mother was a bargirl," I say. "And I do not know if she is alive or dead. That is the truth."

He keeps his eyes on our hands. I do not know if he is really listening to me. His voice goes soft and he says again, "Look."

I do. He strokes his hand gently over mine and then lays it on me so that our fingertips are flared to each side like the wings of a bird. He says, "Our hands look the same."

He says it very softly. Like how sweet this is. The light upon us is red, from the neon, and his hand is very thick and strong and mine is fragile and thin, but suddenly I see what he sees. The moons are the same. That is the first thing I see. He has wide rising moons there at the bottom edges of his fingernails and so do I. Then he slides his hand until our thumbs are beside each other and they are different, of course, in some ways, but there is something else there, a squareness to them around the tip, that we share.

"You see," I say. "I was made for you."

"Yes," he says, very quiet, still studying our hands.

And I think I understand something about the quietness in him. He is sad about the way life seems to him after the war. He is sad about his father and his wife and his mother and all the miles he has to drive because he cannot find something to make life lift him up, light and sweet, and now he finds me and thinks that I am sweet and he lifts for me and we touch. These are good things. This is a good moment, and looking at our hands proves that, for our hands seem somehow to come from the same maker of hands, some maker who is a very fine artist and his work is very clearly his when you see it, even if the subjects are different.

He looks at me now and he smiles, at this sameness, I think, and I ask him, "Did you hear what I said?"

"I'm sorry," he says. "About your . . . mother?"

"Yes."

"What was it you said?"

I take a breath, wishing not to say this once more. "I do not really know if she is dead. She was a bargirl."

"Did she leave you?"

"Yes. When the liberating forces were about to enter the city. She was afraid for her life. She was a bargirl for the Americans."

I feel a little thump of something in me at that. Like hitting a pothole in the dark. But I figure I know what it is. Tien doesn't like what her mama did, and I don't blame her, but I'm guilty of the same sort of thing. If Tien was a little girl feeling bad about her mama taking Americans to bed, I was one of those Americans taking a woman to bed back then who might've been some child's mother. Though I knew Kim wasn't. Still, it was the same sort of thing. That's how I take it. And there is the reminder, too, of the difference in our ages, Tien and me. Not that it bothers me. If it doesn't bother her, it shouldn't bother me. I figure it all out like this. And she's still talking and I'm missing it. But I feel okay now.

"I'm sorry," I say. "Tell me that again."

She starts it over without a pause, without a dirty look, not holding it against me at all that I haven't heard her for a moment. I have no clear memory, but I know this is different from what I was used to, what I came to think was normal from Mattie. That's how my thoughts are running, to things that just make me love Tien more, at each little turn. She says, "She left me with her mother, right here in this apartment. Then she went away. I think she went back to where she grew up. Up near Nha Trang."

"What was your mama's name?" I ask.

When Tien says, "Huong," I'm surprised to feel a quick little letting go of something, though I don't stop to try to figure out why.

"I don't want to talk about her," Tien says.

"Okay," I say.

"She doesn't matter."

"Of course not."

"She never brought me around her men," Tien says.

"She was trying to protect you."

"Yes. You're very sweet to try to let me see it that way."

"It's true," I say.

"She went away for that reason, too. To protect me. She was afraid my father . . ."

Tien stops. I think it is just the pain about him. Her face goes hard and she looks away from me, into the dark of the room, and I figure she's thinking about all the prayers she's made, all the incense she's burned. She's never let go of him. As she sees it, he's still in this room.

Tien says, "She made me lie. All my life. Now to you. I can't even just speak the truth."

"You can always tell me the truth."

She turns back to me. She smiles. She lifts her hand and touches my cheek with her fingertips. "Yes," she says. "My mother went away, too, because she did not want anyone to find out that my father was an American."

"He's dead."

"Yes."

"Your American father."

"Yes. I would not carry a lie this far." Tien nods in the direction of her ancestor shrine. "I pray real prayers."

"Of course."

We fall silent for a time. I feel like pressing this issue and I don't know why. I don't try to figure it out. I just feel the impulse to press her. I say, "How did you learn of his death?"

"He died before I was even born."

"So your mother told you."

"Yes."

I say no more. The impulse suddenly disappears. The street is quiet, I realize. For a long moment there is nothing. The silence buzzes faintly in the room. Then there's the distant brat of a motorbike engine. It grows louder and grates past our window and is gone. After that, there's silence again. It's very late.

Tien says, softly, "Do you think she lied?"

I find my mind slow now. Like I am half asleep. "What?" I say.

"My mother. Do you think she lied?"

It's hard enough, suddenly, just to focus my eyes on Tien. It takes me a few moments to do this.

"About my father dying," she says.

"How would I know?"

"She was a liar."

"Was she?"

"Yes."

"But only for reasons," I say.

"There would be a good reason for that lie."

"What?"

"So I would not have to think about him. So I would not feel abandoned by him. So I would not wonder what she did to make him go away and never want to see her again."

I am very tired now. Very weary. I uncross my legs, turn and sit on the edge of the bed, my side to her.

She says, "Would those not be good reasons for her to tell me this lie?"

"What difference would it make now?"

"None. You are right."

"You wouldn't go to America to try to find him."

"No. Of course not."

"Do you even know his name?"

"She never spoke his name," she says, and there's movement next to me.

I glance and she's sitting beside me now. I let my eyes fall to her breasts. The nipples are dark in this light. They are erect. My hands stir, wanting to touch them, but instead I cross my hands in my lap.

"Do you have a picture of your mother?" I ask, and the question surprises me.

"Yes," she says and she gets up.

I watch her cross the room, her nakedness coursing in me, filling me, in spite of my having made love to her already this very night. I cross my legs to cover myself when she sits down again, a photo in her hand. She scrambles to the other side of the bed and turns on a lamp on the nightstand. She scrambles back, jaundiced by the pale bulb, and I take the photo in my hand, my heart pounding. From her nakedness,

I think. From the nakedness of this woman that I love. I hold the photo for a moment and something in me wants to put it down unseen. Just put it aside and touch Tien again. Right now. Enter her and live forever inside the sweetness of her body, the sweetness of her mind. But I cannot. I have to look at the photo.

It is the photo of a child. Very simple. A girl maybe seven or eight standing in the shadow of a broad-leafed tree that's just off camera. Maybe a banana tree. She isn't posing. She's hardly smiling. She looks up with her deep-cut Asian eyes into the future, at the daughter she will leave at just about this age and at the man this daughter loves. She could be anyone.

Ben looks at my mother and I crouch on the bed behind him and look at her too. I lean against his back, put my hand on his shoulder. He feels very warm. I am suddenly frightened for him. I touch his forehead to see if he has a fever. He does not. But to touch him feels like drawing near a flame.

"She's a child," he says.

"Yes."

"Is this the only photo you have?"

"Yes. My mother destroyed all the photos before she left. She was very frightened. She was a little crazy with the fear."

He looks at my mother's face for a long while.

"You feel very warm," I say.

"Do I?"

"I thought you had a fever."

"She could be anyone," he says.

"I never was frightened for anyone's health before."

"Frightened?"

"When I thought for a moment that you have a fever, I was afraid for you." He reaches up and touches my hand that lies on his shoulder.

"Don't be afraid," he says.

"I am not afraid now," I say. "You have no fever."

He squeezes at my hand. Then he lifts my mother's photo for me to take it. I do. I rise up and I begin to cross the room and all my body prickles from being naked and being seen by this man I love even more than I did a moment ago, just from that little squeeze of my hand and from the way he is surely looking at me from behind as I move. And I take a step away from him and another and I am naked for him and I am feeling heavy now, my limbs are turning again to stone as I take still another step and another and I do not know why, but I am suddenly very conscious of my mother in my hand and I wonder where she is and what she would look like if I could see her right now, with my own adult eyes.

I am before my vanity chest and I bend to the bottom drawer and I open it and I lift the lid on a small lacquer box and I put the picture away. I close the lid and I slide the drawer shut and I turn, expecting to find Ben's eyes upon me. But he is in the bed now, lying with his face to the ceiling, covered to the waist with the sheet.

I cross back to him, still heavy in my legs and a little self-conscious now, feeling exposed. He turns his face at the last moment and sees me and he smiles, with a very soft look in his eyes, and I feel all right again. The past is put back in its box and my body is light and I even stop for him, linger a little, knowing from his eyes that he likes to see me.

"I'm very tired," he says.

"I am too, I think."

"I can stay?"

"Yes. I did not even imagine you would be in some other place tonight."

He smiles again and looks up at the ceiling and closes his eyes. I slip into the bed beside him, covering myself also to the waist, my hip touching his beneath the sheet. I feel for a moment joined to him there, like the place we touch can never be undone, like we are the twins I have read about, who come from their mother's womb with their bodies joined. Brother and sister. Not that I want anything like the feeling of brother and sister with Ben. It is just this connection I imagine in that place on our naked hips.

What I really want is for him to touch me again, even now. Not like brother and sister at all. I want him to touch my secret place again, even though I feel very tender there. It would hurt a little for him to touch me there now, I know, but I want him to do that anyway. And all this makes me think of my mother's urgent words when I brought the story of the beginning of Vietnam to her. There were one hundred sons, she told me. My friend told me that there were fifty boys and fifty girls among the children of the dragon and the princess, and these children grew into adults and they became the ancestors of all the Vietnamese people.

But as I lie beside Ben on this night we make love, I suddenly realize that in the story I have heard in the banyan tree, these brothers and sisters would have had to make love with each other. In this story, all our people began with a brother and a sister lying down naked together and touching and joining their bodies. My mother would not let me think of this. That was behind the heat of her words. But her version of the story only explained the line of our kings. It did not explain where the rest of us came from. In her story, that remained a mystery. But the wives of these kings did not spring from the trees or from the smoke of their fires or from the earth. There had to be more. Surely such a thing as the love between a dragon from the sea and a fairy princess was meant to begin a whole nation and not just put men on a throne. Perhaps this was another of my mother's lies. Perhaps these brothers and sisters lay down together and loved each other.

I shiver at this, like I am suddenly chilled, like there is something crawling just beneath my skin and it is very cold. I have never had a brother or a sister, so the thought of this happening is just between invented people in my head, but even so, it feels very strange to me, it catches in my chest like in the early days of the liberation when the men in the streets with guns would suddenly look at you and you did not know if they recognized that you were just a little girl or they thought you were someone else and they might kill you. I feel like that.

So I turn on my side toward Ben, breaking that place on our hips where he and I are joined, and I put my hand on his chest and I want to move my hand down to the place where we have been joined like the children of the dragon and the princess, the brothers and sisters who knew no shame from the blood between them. But I do not move my hand. Not right now. I am glad to hold back

and know that I could do this thing at any moment. He
will sleep beside me and I will sleep and I could wake at
any moment in the night and touch him there. Knowing I
can touch him and holding back is a sweet thing. That odd
warmth that feels like fear, fades away. Ben's arm comes
around my shoulders and draws me tighter against him. I
say, "Why did you come here?"

There's an answer in my head right away, to this. Like
almost everything that's been going on inside me since
Tien and I made love, this answer just comes on me and
it's like I'm sitting back waiting to see what it is, myself.
Things come into me and I don't know from where. I say,
"I think it was to find you."

This answer puzzles her as much as it does me. She says,
"You knew?"

"I didn't know a thing," I say. And I wait a moment to
see what I mean. I look hard into the dark above us. A
gecko is motionless in a shadow, just outside a stripe of
neon, waiting for something he knows is coming along.
I feel the warmth of the palm of her hand on my chest,
the press of her body inside the circle of my arm. She
seems so familiar. I think I feel that briefly. But that would

happen now and then on the road. I'd slide into a town somewhere and I'd never been there in my life but it was familiar. I take it like that. I say, "I mean it was supposed to happen this way somehow."

"Do you think so?"

"Yes," I say.

"Do you think something like a god brought you here?"

I should have expected her to take what I said this way. It's natural. But this is far beyond the point I think I'm making. "I don't know," I say. "I think I'm just saying things that come into my head. Things people are supposed to say when they talk like this."

"I am not familiar with this custom."

"But I think I believe what I'm saying, too. About us."

"I was brought up a Buddhist," Tien says. "Not a very good one. My mother wasn't very religious. How could she be and do what she did in her life? My grandmother believed in her dead husband's spirit, and the spirit of her father. But that's not really Buddhism. That's something the Chinese oppressors brought us a thousand years ago."

"Does Buddhism explain why I'm here?" I ask.

"I do not think so," she says. "Buddhism says that all the suffering in the world comes from desire."

I draw Tien closer to me, sliding my hand down to the point of her hip, letting her skin run softly into my hand and up my arm and into my head. I want things to be clear for me now, about her, about what this all means. Too much is going on in me that I wasn't expecting. It feels like there's something waiting in the shadow for me to come along. "Are you suffering now?" I ask her.

"From my desire for you?"

"Yes."

"I said I was not a very good Buddhist."

"It's only the good Buddhists that suffer from desire?"

"They suffer from the desire not to feel desire."

"This is better, isn't it?"

"Yes," she says, and her hand slides down my stomach and onto that place that is slack now and quiet but I stir at her touch. And almost at once the night begins to blur at its edges, just when I think I'd be waking up in my head like I seem to be doing in my body, the darkness above me billows like mill smoke and the gecko disappears and I suddenly want to let go of all I can see and hear and feel against me. I say, "I'm very tired now, Tien," and her hand stops.

"Is it okay?" she asks. "That I touch you?"

"Of course," I say.

"Will we sleep now?"

"I think so."

"Can you say this thing once more before we do?"

"Yes. And you?"

"I will."

"I love you," I say and I know I mean it, though this time the words come hard. From this sudden weariness. From that, I decide, because I feel the deep sea-wave of sleep rolling under me and lifting me into the dark and I don't even hear her say the words back to me.

And I wake in bright sun. I remember a brief moment when she kissed me good-bye. She was up early for her work and I was deep in a dreamless sleep and her lips woke me, on my cheek, on my brow, then on my mouth and I put my arm around her and she was in Saigontour-ist clothes and I smelled her makeup and she said, "I will come to you this evening." Then she was gone and I blurred back into sleep.

And now I'm awake and it's late in the morning. The roar of motorbikes fills the room and I sit up. The sheet is twisted away from me and I'm naked and I think of Tien's kiss, how she might have seen me lying here in my nakedness. I stir at this. And at once my hands go out to the sheet and scrabble at the knots and pull the cloth over me. This odd surge of modesty in an empty room seems to come directly from my hands and I look at them as if they could explain.

Then I try to doze again, but I cannot. I rise up finally and I am naked for a moment in the middle of the room, in the sunlight, and again I feel unsettled by this, again my hands drive me to cover myself. I put on my pants and my shirt and I'm breathing hard. Like I'm on a drug or something. Like something is in my body. I look around as if there'd be some proof from the night before. A mirror on a tabletop and a dusting of powder, the butt end of a reefer. Something. Anything. Though I know we weren't even drunk, Tien and me. I know there's been nothing in this room but the feeling between us. And that is unaffected by this sudden mood. I see her silk pantaloons on a chair and these same hands of mine that have wanted to cover me stir now with the memory of her skin on their palms, they feel the cool run of her flesh on them, right now. But still there is something.

I finish dressing and go out of her rooms, closing the door softly, leaning there a moment, wondering at all of this. And then I go along the outer balcony and it smells of fish sauce and wood fire and there's a jumble of red tile roofs and straw mats and hanging laundry and the clucking of chickens from somewhere down the alley, and as I pass by an old woman crouching near the metal circle of stairs, she nods at me and puts a fold of betel leaf in her mouth.

I go down the stairs and out into the street and I seek the sun, stay out of the shade. I walk along the street for a long way in the sun, taking it in hard and straight on my face and my arms, trying to sweat this feeling away. Then at last I hail a pedicab and the driver asks where I want

to go and I don't know. I think of my hotel, but I don't
want the empty room again, the empty bed, the paddle
fan moving the wet air, and so I say the Hotel Rex, which
is down near the circular fountain at Le Loi and Nguyen
Hue.

I sit in the pedicab's open chair, the driver out of sight
behind me, and there is nothing before my eyes but the
street full of Vietnamese people rushing past on their
motorbikes and I move as if in a dream, floating in this
street that looks just like it did years ago, in 1966. How
many years ago? I shape that question in just those words
in my head and I expect it simply to be the prompter of
a bit of elementary math—I'm talking to myself in my
head in some simpleminded way—but with that question
comes another question and it surprises me, it's unwilled,
it's from some ongoing self-interrogation that's deeper,
darker, and the question is: how old is Tien? Why should
the one question lead to the other? I pose this to myself
and do not want an answer, I lean forward, try just to float
here in this street, like in a lovely dream, yes, try to sense
the tamarind trees joining overhead, try to drift through
their shadows knowing I can wake at any moment, but
she's on my skin, this woman I love, she's burning in me
like incense, and the question slides forward again, even
though there's no past to reckon with, all the women I've
ever known, as few as they are, have faded from me, it's

as if they never existed, and she has said I love you to a man three times in her life and it was only me, I am that man. Except the math is this: twenty-eight years. She can be very close to that age and it has been twenty-eight years since I've been in these same streets, since I've gone to a bar in the very street where Tien once lived with her bargirl mother.

Her mother Huong. The woman I met and loved was Kim. Perhaps Huong's friend. Perhaps there was this wonderful crossing of paths. Perhaps one hot afternoon I was drinking in the bar with Kim and she drifted to the back of the place, to the little room behind a curtain, where they kept a shrine with incense and fruit for the woman who once owned the bar, a woman killed one night on the street in front by a drunken Army man, and her picture was there in the center of the shrine—I remember her now, her face in a photo in the center of the shrine—and she had no family to pray for her and so her girls prayed for her, my Kim and all the other girls, and perhaps one hot afternoon the girls curled up in the booths and in the back room and took their naps but Kim was with me and so she stayed awake, drinking with me, and she stepped through the curtain and perhaps Huong was there. Perhaps I followed Kim and before me was this other bargirl whose name, Huong, I've long forgotten, and perhaps her blouse was open and a baby girl was

nursing at Huong's nipple, an infant, and perhaps this
infant was Tien.

I float now in the shadows of the tamarinds with this
thought. The girls in white ao dais race past on their
motorbikes and I close my eyes and I cannot remember
such a thing happening, the nursing baby at the breast of
Kim's friend, but it might have. I could have stood before
Tien's mother with my own bargirl lover and seen the
infant Tien suckling at a breast that I might have paid to
suckle at, easily, if I had not been with Kim instead. And
at this thought I feel a sweet rush of guilt. Sweet, yes,
sweet. Sweet with relief. A thing like this is what has been
troubling me. A thing like this. I am this much older than
Tien. I have been this sort of man, who has paid to sleep
with a woman like her sort of mother. Sweet guilt. These
are my sins. Only these.

I pass him in the street and he does not see me. I am in my
Saigontourist car with Mr. Thu the driver and in the backseat are a man and woman who are husband and wife from
Germany. Ben is in a xich lo and a very old man is pedaling
him through the street. I see him and I am in the middle
of telling the German couple something or other about Ho

Chi Minh City and I stop what I am saying right away. I turn to see my Ben who is leaning forward in his seat and his eyes are closed so that he does not see me and the old man is wearing a straw hat and I begin to roll down my window. I would put my body halfway out of the car and call to my Ben, but he is gone too soon, the window is not even all the way down. I laugh. He was looking so sweet, his eyes closed, and I think that his thoughts are about me.

I turn to the German couple. We are speaking English because they speak it well and so do I and our German-speaking guide is off with a busload from Berlin, and I say to the man and the woman, who are perhaps fifty years old, "I am sorry. I saw someone I know passing by."

They nod and look out the window as if they would recognize right away who I mean.

"It is a man," I say and the German woman turns her face to me and smiles.

I want to say to her, I know what you feel with this man who sits beside you. We are women, you and I, and we lie with a man we love and we open our bodies and we love these men with some parts of us that only they know about and I think that they do not even know that they know.

I want to say these things to her as we smile at each other, one woman to another woman. But instead I say

that in the two thousand square kilometers of Ho Chi
Minh City, more than five million people are living. Her
smile fades and she looks at me thoughtfully. Her husband is looking at me now again, too. I am trying to be
the tour guide once more. I think of those five million
people and I want to speak of the great advances in hous-
ing and employment that our revolutionary government
is making but I am really thinking of the half of those
five million who are women and how they must all yearn
to have what I now have, this kind of love. I look at
this German woman's face and she and her husband are
sitting with a wide space between them, each pressed
against a window, and I have not seen them touch on
this day, though we have been in the Ben Thanh Market and in a pagoda and in the Military Museum where
a man and a woman who loved each other very much
would surely think to touch, since the museum itself—I
am ashamed to say this but it is true—is very boring.
And I think that no one in this city, not one of the two
and a half million women here, or any of the women in
Germany either, for that matter, has ever felt what I am
feeling. But they want to, they want the secret places of
their bodies to feel as sweetly sore from the attentions
of love as mine does, they want their breaths to catch
as mine does and their bodies to strive to leap through
a car window as mine does at the sight of the man who

has lain with them, even if he is gone in a moment and he is dozing or dreaming in the care of an old man with a straw hat. That such an odd and simple thing as this should bring such joy, they must all want that and not be able to have it. That is perhaps a selfish and reactionary thing to think, but in this moment it seems true or else these two people in the backseat would be pressed against each other even then and every woman on the street would be rushing in wild distraction to leap into the arms of the man she loves.

But, of course, I am doing no such thing at the moment. I laugh at myself for all these thoughts. The husband and the wife both wrinkle their brows at me.

"I am sorry," I say.

For a moment I have no idea what to do with my body. I stand before the Rex Hotel and I should he doing something, I should turn one way or another and I should make my legs move, I should go somewhere, into the hotel, perhaps—I think I came here for the rooftop bar—or off in some direction along the street, perhaps now back to my own hotel. But I have no impulse at all. Nothing. I do ache for the night to come and to be back in Tien's bed. That's very clear. But all the moments between this one on the street and that one, still hours away, are unimaginable to me.

And still, I know that things are much better inside me. That's the very reason I have this sudden emptiness. The thing that had been growling in the dark in me is silent, but the guilt that took its place was an old one and faded away at once. I'm not proud of the way my life has gone. I knew that long ago. So if Tien in some strange way was present in the past I'm ashamed of, then that's okay. If she was, she was there as a brief glimpse of a purity and innocence that would someday return to me in the form of a woman and make me whole.

And standing on the sidewalk on this morning in Vietnam in 1994, I think: what it must mean is, I've been forgiven. If there is some higher power in the universe that gives a damn about guilt and shame and forgiveness, then surely for Tien and me to be brought together like this and to be made to touch like this and to feel like this—especially if she's the child of a bargirl herself, especially if I saw her for one ignorant moment in that former life of mine—if such a power exists, then surely, for all this to happen, it shows that I've been forgiven.

This is what I think for a few sweet moments. And then I decide to go back to my hotel and lie on my bed and think about Tien until it is time to go to her again. And so I cross the street into the plaza before the Rex.

A photographer lopes up and motions for me to turn so that the City Hall and Ho Chi Minh's statue will be behind me and I wave him away. A girl with handfuls of postcards takes his place, following me step for step as I move down the plaza now, heading for the fountain at the traffic circle, and I wave her away too. And then the little man with the mustache is at my side and I recognize him as the pimp on the motorcycle and he's speaking low to me.

"You want nice Vietnam girl? Boom boom all day all night?" he says.

"No," I say and he doesn't turn away, he continues to follow me and I wonder what it is about me that he won't believe what I've said.

"She is very nice," he says. "Do anything for you."

"No," I say again and I try to make it sharper but I'm not sure it is and I know there's no desire for another woman, a faint shudder runs in me at the thought of touching any woman but Tien now, and that makes me happy, but the very happiness of it turns at once to a dark thing and I know I've been thinking about bargirls too much, that's what's going on, this is connecting to all of that, and I want to rush away from this man but I can't make my legs go any faster.

"Here is she," he says, and I look and we're moving toward the motorbike parked at the curb and the girl is there, perched on the back of the seat, and she's very young and her hair that was rolled up when I saw her before is unpinned now, falling long and dark, over her shoulder and down over her breast. She is looking at me with steady eyes, looking into my eyes.

I stop. If there's a moment in a body that's the opposite of sexual desire, this is a thing that is happening to me now, like driving in a fog and not daring to stop on the shoulder because you know someone will crash into you from behind and not seeing enough even to find an exit ramp and knowing you can only go forward and knowing something is waiting out there that you won't see until you slam into it and your body squeezes hard to make you very small and you feel it most in your penis and in your balls, they suck in and clench tight, and it's like that, seeing this woman waiting for me to take her to a loveless bed.

"She is my sister," the man with the mustache says. "She is one virgin. You say hello to her. Her name Kim."

I turn to him. "Kim?" I don't know what's in my voice but the man flinches.

"Sure," he says, but it's meek, a child caught in a lie. "You no like name Kim?"

Whatever surprised the man in my voice is kicking up inside me now. I'm clenching tighter. Some shape in the fog ahead. I start to turn away and his hand is on my arm.

"Wait," he says. "She not Kim. That name Americans like, so we say she name Kim."

I stop. He angles his face around trying to look me in the eyes. He laughs a little laugh that is full of something that sounds like respect.

"You know already. You know Vietnam. I see you smart GI vet. Her name Ngoc. American like Kim better."

I want to tell him to shut up. I'm not looking at him and keeping my face turned is just making him say more. I force my eyes to go to him and when I do he smiles broadly and he cuffs me on the arm.

"You smart man," he says. "All Vietnam good-time girl name Kim."

Now she is near me. "My name Ngoc," she says. "I do for you special."

It is ten minutes until six o'clock and I get out of the car and I say good-bye to Mr. Thu over my shoulder. I am thinking of my heart, how I can feel it rushing inside me. I look to the little table where I first see him, and some men of Vietnam are in that place drinking beers and then I am in the shadow of the alleyway that leads to my rooms.

I go up the iron stairs and I pass women crouching and playing Chinese cards. I say hello to these women every night but I say nothing now. I am sorry for that, but Ben has filled me up and he has squeezed all my words out and he is squeezing also at my chest, making it difficult to breathe, and I am loving this feeling.

My door is unlocked, this is the way I leave it always, I tell him so just last night, so when I push open the door I am ready to be in his arms. But he is not there. I stop. I stand in the middle of the room. I look around. The sheets are thrown back. Like he has risen only just a few moments ago and he has gone into the kitchen or into the bathroom. I go to the kitchen door and the room is empty. The water drips from the faucet into my metal pan. The sound is very loud. There is no other sound. I step to the bathroom door and I know already that he is not there. The door is open and I can see this clearly. I move back to the center of the room where I live and I look to the ancestor shrine. The incense is cold. The fruit is turning dark. No face is there, either. A rooster crows somewhere out in the alley, far away. He does not like how the light is going from the sky.

I try not to think of my father. I tell myself: Ben is not gone forever. It is not fair to think of my father because of him. For one thing, Ben will come up the stairs and along the balcony and through that door any moment. For another thing, my father is dead. He did not leave me forever without another thought, he is simply dead. And perhaps his spirit did not leave me at all. Perhaps I drew him here with my prayers long ago and he has all these years been very grateful to me for supporting him in the afterlife, as we are supposed to do for our dead ancestors, and he has wept ghostly tears because he was not able to come back to Vietnam as a man, as a father, and find his daughter. These are the things scrambling around in me as I stand here. Thoughts like these.

But I am afraid there may be more. My face and hands have gone cold now. My heart is still rushing, but for some new reason. I stand halfway between the empty bed and the empty shrine and the beats of my heart are like pebbles, piling up, filling my chest and pushing up now into my throat. I must move from this place where I am standing. This much I know.

I turn my body around. It is very heavy. I push against it and I am moving to the bathroom. I go in and I pull on the chain and a light comes from the bare bulb into the room, a light like on those late nights when I would lie in my mother's bed and she would rise and go into the bathroom and I would be awake—as soon as she rose and left me alone there, I would wake—and she would go in and pull the bathroom door just partway closed and turn the light on and there would be only silence for the longest time and I do not know what it was that she was doing.

I lift my hands to my blouse buttons and I begin to undo them. This feels good. My hands rush now. I strip off my blouse and throw it down at my feet and I unsnap my bra and it falls away and my nipples awake at their sudden nakedness. I think this will bring him through the door. I slip off my shoes and I unzip my skirt and I dig my thumbs deep into these daylight layers of me and I drag the skirt and my panty hose and my underwear off all at once, stepping quickly from the clinging toes, and I am naked now, completely naked, and the secret lips of me pout for him and I reach up to my hair and pull out pins, throwing them down, my fingers trembling until my hair is tumbling over my shoulders and down my back.

I listen for the door. There are motorbikes distant in the street and the laughter of the women playing cards, and I listen to the place in front of those sounds, I wait for the sound of the door. But there is nothing. Except, now, a child crying somewhere nearby, passing, just outside, and then the child is gone, and the women are silent now, and there are only the motorbikes. But the door does not open. And it is all right, because I am not clean. It is good that Ben is late. This is what I tell myself.

I run the water into my plastic tub and I crouch beside it and I take my sponge and I soap it up with the soap that says it is 99 and 44 one-hundreds percent pure. I am far less pure than that now. But it does not bother me to think so. There is another kind of pureness possible, I think. A pureness that happens when he fills me with the part of his body I still have not looked at. I will look at that part tonight. I rub the soap beneath my arms, around my breasts, down to the place on my body that is his alone to touch. I wash myself and rinse with fresh water and I rise and I dry myself with soft pats of my towel. He would be that gentle if he were here to dry me now. I touch myself with the towel just as Ben would.

Then I reach for my silk robe hanging on the back of the door, but my hand hesitates and falls. I realize that I like being naked. He will be happy to find me naked when he comes through the door.

I step into the room. I have not done my prayers. I think to take that robe now and do this thing for my father. But I do not. I want to remain naked. My eyes fill with tears, and this surprises the part of me trying to figure all this out. I know I want Ben to hurry now. I know I am afraid he will not come here. I am afraid he has gotten on an airplane and gone back across the sea and he will forget me and I will wait naked in this room all night and all day tomorrow and the next tomorrow and the next until they find me dead here like this. If there is something more to these tears, or to this trembling that wishes to start in my hands, I am not ready to think of that. It is surely enough for now that I am afraid Ben has left me.

I could light just the incense. He deserves not to have to wait for that. I move toward the shrine and then I stop and my face grows hot and my hands fall to cover me and the trembling has begun in them and it is because I think he can see me like this. My father can. I have been naked in this room many times before, of course, and it never occurred to me that he was here. But surely I knew. I would pray, my nakedness covered, but barely, by my silk robe, I would let loose the smoke of the incense like a lover looses her hair, and I would finish and rise from where I knelt and turn, and many times I would let the robe fall from me at once. It is often very hot in this room and the air is thick with rain that has died and turned into spirit and has filled the air unseen, like my father. And at those times my words had hardly faded from the room—he was still here where I called him to be—and I exposed my naked woman's body, and so it was for him. I turn and hurry into the bathroom and close the door and I lean against it. Do I truly believe these things? Has my father lived with me all these years, watching? Did he see me touch Ben last night? Did he see my nakedness just now?

"Go away," I say, aloud. Gently. I do not want to hurt his feelings. "Please," I say. "I want a living man."

I wait to see if he will go. I cannot tell.

And then I hear Ben coming in, the latch lifting, the hinges creaking.

I turn and I throw open this door and Ben is there. I am no longer ashamed in my nakedness. Because of him. He has taken any shame in this away from me. He is caught there, the door closing behind him, his hand still on the latch, his face turning now to my sudden appearance. He straightens and faces me. His eyes are wide and sad. I move quickly to him and I open my arms and I leap up for him to catch me and clutch me to him, knowing he will, and he does, his arms cross my back and press me hard against him as my legs go around his waist.

"Oh my god," he says.

I think he says these words because he is so happy for me to be like this in his arms. I want him to carry me about the room, to spin with me and dance with me, holding me off the ground. But he does not move. He holds me close to him and he is breathing heavily, I can feel him, I put my face against the side of his throat and I wait and I can feel his heart there and it is beating very fast. I pull at his shirt. Pull it up out of his pants so that the part of me that only he knows can kiss at his skin. The cloth rumples across me there, a button touches me like a fingertip and is

gone, then there is the mat of hair on his stomach against
me and in all of this I am like a woman I never knew
I could be, a woman so free like this about her body. I
know very clearly that in this feeling I am being counterrevolutionary, my country would be ashamed of me. But
I do not care. I am free, I am perched here high on a tree
and I need only to leap one more time in order to fly, and
it is because of him. And this is a strange and contradic-
tory thing: clinging to him, I feel I can fly; devoted to him
completely, I feel free.

"I love you," I say.

"You're a woman," he says, very softly.

I know at once what he means. I let go of him with
my legs and I climb down to stand on my own feet. He is
right, and he is the man I love, to say this thing to me. I
want to walk beside him to the bed. In Vietnam we have
a society where men and women share their work equally
and they should share their bed equally, and I am surprised that this man raised from childhood by an imperialist government can know this. It makes me want to jump
up on him again.

"I love your smile," he says, touching my cheek with
his fingertips. It would be hard to explain the thing I have
just smiled about, so I simply turn my face and kiss the
fingertips that have touched me and then I take the hand
in mine and bring it to my side and I tug at him so that

we can walk together across the room to the place where we will make love.

He yields, he moves, but he feels very heavy. We go to the bed and he stops me before we lie down and he pulls me to him and presses me close. There is something in him, some feeling I do not understand. A quick dark thing is rushing into my head, and I say, "Is it only my smile?"

I feel his head move. He is looking at me, trying to see into my eyes, but I keep my face against his chest. I want the answer to this question first. Then I realize he does not understand what I mean. Still not looking at him I say, "Is it only my smile that you love?"

"No," he says.

"I am sorry to ask this," I say. "I am still a selfish girl."

"It's not selfish," he says. "I thought we settled that last night."

"And now I am sorry again. I should say I am a selfish *woman*. We settle that only one minute ago."

He holds me gently away from him and we look into each other's eyes. I want very much for us to make love now.

I let go and curl backward onto the bed, propped up a little with the pillow against the wall, and he eases down beside me. But he does not lie beside me, he does not touch me, he sits there as if he's waiting for something to happen, something to be said. I wait, too. The light is fading in the room.

Then, when the motorbikes out in the street are filling my head like my own fears, rushing with a nasty sound around and around the block and not going anywhere, I say, "I guided a husband and a wife from Germany today. I do not think they love each other."

And he says, very low, "Can I ask you some questions?"

I say, "Quickly. Please."

"How old are you?"

"Twenty-six," I say.

He lifts his chin just a little bit, thinking something out.

Suddenly I believe I understand. I say, "You're not too old. Vietnam girls respect an older man."

He turns to me.

"More than respect," I say. "A Vietnam girl can respect an older man and she can feel passion for him, too."

"You sound like my mother again. The way you explain yourself."

"It's okay that way too. Think of me like I am forty-six."

He smiles. "No. I'm too old. That's good. Too many years have gone."

I am not understanding again.

"It's 1994," he says. "I was here in 1966. Don't you see? That's twenty-eight years."

Yes?"

"You're twenty-six."

I am lost. I concentrate on these numbers that seem so important to him and there is a hissing in my head, some little sound from a dark corner in me, but I try to think only about the numbers. I say, "Almost twenty-seven."

There is a little flinch in him, a catching. "Twenty-seven? Yes? All right. It's still all right."

"It's all right," I say. "We are closer in age. That's good too, isn't it?"

"When is your birthday?"

"May 15."

"May? Next month?"

"Yes."

"Look," he says, almost sharply. "It's all right. Really."

"I know," I say.

"I was here in 1966." Then he hesitates. "I came in February. I left after a year. It was 1967."

I wait for him. He is thinking hard again. I am not thinking at all. I do not feel comfortable with numbers. The hissing has stopped. Then he turns to me abruptly.

"Tien," he says. "Please tell me about how you know your father is dead."

"My mother told me this thing. When she left me with my grandmother."

"Your mother told you."

"Yes. She did not want to, I think. But my grandmother made her."

"She didn't want to. Good. That's good."

"Why is that good?"

"Your grandmother knew that he was dead?"

"Yes."

"Did she talk about this, too?"

I try to think. "I can't remember. I don't think so."

"Then you don't know what your grandmother knew. Was she there when your mother told you?"

"No."

"Your mother could have lied."

"We spoke of this last night."

"I'm sorry," he says.

I put my hand on his shoulder. "Is this the thing that worries you?"

"Yes."

"Why?" I ask this and for a moment it is still like I do not know the answer. All through these words we speak to each other on the bed, I have played the fool to myself. Now he simply fixes his eyes on me and I know. His brown eyes like mine. I grab the hand with the fingertips like mine. I have gone cold. There is a tumbling in me. I lean forward, my head goes down, I thump into his chest, my forehead there, and I pull back instantly. Suddenly I cannot touch him, and that is not a thing I can live with, I know that at once, the hissing has returned and it fills my lungs, this sound, and I cannot breathe.

"What?" he says. "Do you know something?"

I know nothing. This is *his* fear, I cry to myself. It can't be true. It isn't true.

"What is it?" he says.

I can barely shape words now. "Tell me your worry. Now. Please. I have this thought. A terrible thing. Tell me."

God forgive me, all I want to do is put these things aside and touch her. I should have done that when I first came through the door. She is a woman. She is not my child. She is no one's child.

But perhaps no forgiveness is necessary. I haven't figured out the months exactly, but it feels wrong. The time feels wrong. And how could we meet like this? How could we feel like this if it was true? But she deserves to know my fear. For the sake of all the love I feel for Tien, I can't keep such a secret from her, even if it's a foolish thing, as insubstantial as a dream I would wake from out on the road, sleeping in my rig in a rest stop in the middle of some dark night and I wake and I can't even remember what it was only seconds ago that made my heart pound like this and made this cry come from my mouth but there is only the smell of the earth and hay and the vinyl of the truck cab and there's just the tick of metal and a wind rush of some semi going by trying to make up time. There was never anything left of a fear like that, whatever it'd been, after I sat up and shook my head.That's all it will take now.

I say, "When I was here during the war, I was . . . with a woman."

"With her? You mean you sleep with a Vietnamese woman?"

"Yes."

"Was she a bargirl, this woman?"

"Yes."

Tien draws the sheet up around her. I've not been looking at her body. Not till I can just put this thing away for good. But I regret her gesture now. I'm anxious to get this over with.

"That was long ago," I say. "Please."

"Before I was born."

"Yes. A year before. More than that."

"More than a year?"

"Yes."

"Then . . . Oh, Ben, I am a foolish girl."

She throws back the sheet and puts her arms around me. I hold her close. I lay my hands on the bareness of her back.

She says, "I think a terrible thing."

"It's what I was thinking."

She pulls back, looks at me. "How can this be?"

"It can't. I don't think. I'm not sure about the time. Should we stop and figure it out carefully?"

"Why should you think this? There were many bargirls for the American imperialist army in this city."

"Please."

She puts her hand over her mouth. "I am sorry."

"It's okay."

She lowers her face. "This time it was not the state speaking."

"No?"

"It was my jealousy."

"Tien. Listen to me. What there is between us . . . I've never felt this way before. Not for a bargirl. Not even for my wife."

"Is this true?"

"Yes, my darling."

She rises up on her knees. Her nipples pass in front of my eyes, dark in the fading light, and they stir me, instantly. I yearn to touch my lips there. And now only the tiniest dropping of my eyes and I can see her softest place. I am nearly ready to do what I should have done when I first came into this room tonight.

She says, "Hands can look alike. There are only so many hands."

"Yes," I say.

"With so many girls. So many. For her to be the same, the girl who was my mother, the girl who was . . . What was she for you? This was a one-time girl?"

"No."

"Two times? Three?"

I can hear her voice going tight. "Please. I'm about to turn into the evil imperialist power again."

"Sorry." She sinks back down to sit on the bed, though she doesn't draw the sheet around her. I find myself trying to keep my eyes on her face once more. She says, "Did you love her?"

"I thought so."

"Did she get pregnant?"

"Not that I know of. No. No, she didn't."

"Then I cannot be . . . what you feared."

"No."

"Please," she says. "Can we make love now?"

My hands move to hers, take them. But I remember our fingers lying beside each other last night, the moons echoing, echoing. Was Kim pregnant? "I want to be entirely honest," I say, trying to remember when it was that Kim and I parted. "I don't know if she was pregnant. I met her a while after I came here. Perhaps in May. When I left Vietnam I hadn't seen her for a few months. So . . . I don't know."

"You met her in May?"

"Yes."

"May 1966?"

"Yes."

"Then it was not more than a year."

"What wasn't?"

"Before I was born. When you slept with this bargirl."

The thrashing begins. A physical thing, in my chest, in my throat. A thing in my head, too, now that the math has betrayed me. The two years between Tien and Kim are gone.

"I know," Tien says. "You ask me her name last night, my mother. I tell you her name. This is a simple thing, is it not? Was this girl you sleep with named Huong?"

And now I am back to this. The thing that drove me nearly mad this afternoon. I say, "She called herself Kim," and I watch Tien carefully. Her face instantly softens. She smiles.

She says, "You see? There is nothing to this fear."

I have another chance, another clean chance just to go on with the rest of my life loving this woman sitting naked here before me.

Then she begins to explain her earlier words, to fix the tiniest misimpression. "I do not mean to criticize your life," she says. "When you were here as a member . . . See? I am about to speak of imperialist powers again. When you were here in 1966, you were a young man, a lonely man, a frightened man. I am glad you had a beautiful Vietnam girl to hold close to you. It prepared you for me? Yes?" She laughs lightly at this and already I am having trouble. I hear my mother's manner in her and I'm crying out inside my head: this is not genetic, something like this, this is a learned thing. But then she laughs and she lifts her face and I even see something in her face, all of a sudden, I'm not sure what, something around her mouth, her chin, something. I turn my face sharply away from her.

I feel her hand on my shoulder. She says, "I am not laughing at you."

"I know," I say, moving my shoulder just a little bit, trying to make the gesture small, gentle, when it wants to be big, when I want suddenly to jump up and throw myself through that window Why? Why? It's my imagination now, I tell myself. There's nothing in her face. The way she explains herself can't come from her blood. But I do say, "Was your mother ever called anything else? Around the bar?"

"I did not go around the bar."

"You never heard a man call her . . ."

"No."

"If I told you half the bargirls in Saigon called themselves Kim to the men they . . ."

"I would tell you to shut up now. Half the bargirls in Saigon still would have been twenty-five thousand bargirls. My mother's name is Huong. She calls herself Huong."

I am crying now. I say, "She holds some American GI in her arms and makes him feel like he is not about to die, makes him feel he is not alone in the world. That is okay, that is not making her an enemy of the state, that is a woman who can love a man very easy, can give him something worth a million times more than the few dollars he gives her because he wants her and needs her and so she can feed her child and her mother."

Ben takes me into his arms. He rises to his knees and he lifts me, naked. These words have surprised me. The feeling in my body surprises me too. I understand. The way my body feels opened up: that secret part of me of course, but also the rest—my nipples, a place in the

center of my chest, the palms of my hands, the soles of
my feet—there is this gaping in me, a hungry space, I
want to draw Ben into me like those dark stars they speak
of, the stars you cannot even see in the telescopes because
they burn black and they want to draw all the rest of the
universe into them. Suddenly I understand my mother,
I think, a little bit, the thing she might have felt with a
man. I understand the men, too, the best of them perhaps, someone like Ben.

He says, "It's still one chance in twenty-five thousand,
isn't it?"

"It is no chance," I say, and as soon as I say it, I do
not believe it. As soon as I say it, I flare hot and all the
strength goes from me and I lean into him and the tears
are still flowing and as weak as I feel now, my chest begins
to heave and I can hear myself sobbing.

"Tien," he says. "Darling," he says. He holds me tight
and I so much want his nakedness upon me but I am also
afraid of it now. And I suddenly know what is happening in this room. It is my father's ghost. He is a jealous
man. He has been curling the invisible smoke of his soul
around us, making us breathe him in, and he has wisped
his way into our brains, filled us with these fears to keep
us apart.

I clench at these sobs, stuff them back down in my
throat, I go hard now. I will not show him my tears. Not

again. I wept for him for years. I knelt before his shrine
and I prayed for his soul and I burned the incense and
offered him food and a place for his soul to rest so that
it would not wander the land of the dead in loneliness
and fear. I was a bargirl to him. I did not offer my body
but I offered everything else. More than my body. He
was an American GI and he was in a foreign place and
I held him close with my prayers and my smoke and I
said, Do not be afraid, do not be lonely. And this is how
he repays me.

My eyes are dry. I lift my face to Ben. I will hold only
this man now. My hands go to the buttons on his shirt
and I am whispering to Ben without speaking: Do not
stop me, please my darling, put these fears aside, they are
from my father speaking to us, my true father who cannot
bear to let me go to another man, please my darling let
me touch you now.

And Ben does not stop me. I lean forward into him,
pulling at the sleeves of his shirt, hugging him and stripping the shirt from him in the same gesture. And in my
mind I am speaking now to my father: See this. See what I
do. See my nakedness and the nakedness of my lover. You
must accept this or I will never say another word to the
gods for you.

I feel the sheet over my ankles and my feet, and I kick
it away. I want no part of my body to be covered. I do not

care if my father is watching. I will show him all of my nakedness and he will know it is not for him but for this man I love. I square around and I am pulling at the belt on Ben's pants. My hands tremble. The belt will not yield. Ben's hands come down and they cover mine, hold me still for a moment, and I am afraid he will stop this again. "Please," I say.

His hands hesitate. Then he puts mine aside and pulls open the belt and then the button on his pants and the zipper goes down and my own hands help his, my thumbs hook inside his underpants and I am helping him pull all of that off him at once. I sense his nakedness, catch the faintest sideways glimpse of the dangle of him. But I do not look. Not yet. He turns his back and he bends and he takes off his socks and he is naked and I lie back on the bed and he comes over me and I put my hands on his bare back and I draw his full weight onto me, kissing his mouth, wanting his mouth to yield, to give me that opening into him. But his lips stay closed. They are kind to me. They are soft. They kiss me on the lips, on the cheek, but they stay closed. And then his face moves to the side of mine, his body shifts and slides off the top of me. I cling to him. I will not let him separate from me. And he does not. He stops. But his arms stay about me. His body presses against my side. His face comes to my throat, buries itself there. I hold him. I am breathing very fast. My throat is tight.

I look toward the ceiling of my room. I look for a face there that I have never seen. I think I might be able to see it now. I want to speak aloud to him. But I cannot explain this to Ben. Still, I do not need to say the words for my father to hear them. If he is in my head giving me these fears, and in Ben's head, then he can hear me like this, and I say to him, Go away. Go away now and never return. Go find the woman you loved. Be with her. She is alive somewhere. Go to her and live on her prayers for a while.

I move my hand. I have not seen that part of Ben yet. I will wait until the time is ours alone. But I move my hand. I hope my father is watching. I should feel shame at that, but I do not. I move my hand and I reach and I lay my palm against the point of Ben's hip. He is lying on his side facing me. His arm is around me and his hand is on me, just below my breasts. His lips are pressed against the side of my throat. I wonder if he can feel my heart there. It is beating fast for him, for the thing I want to do. I move my hand over his hip and across the tight curls of his hair and I open my hand wide, like my mouth wanting a deep kiss, and he is in my palm and my fingers softly curl around this part of him that I am not ashamed for the ghost of my father to see me touch but that I have trouble speaking a word for.

Penis means nothing to me. *Cock* means nothing to me. In my language this part is *ngọc hành,* a word that is acceptable for a person to say if there is a good reason, but when I hear this word as a girl I am very puzzled, for it is made up of two words: *ngọc,* which means a gem or a precious stone, and *hành,* which means an onion. These things contradict each other, it has always seemed to me. And neither thing is what I am touching now with my own hand, with my own will and my own desire. The street word for this male part, the word that my friend would whisper in the hidden place inside the banyan tree where we would talk, is *cu,* a word that it is not acceptable to say. It means turtledove. And this is the word now. Ben's secret part is a turtledove to me, a fragile thing, a soft thing, very soft, and it moves in my hand, a bird caught sleeping in its dark nest and I feel a very tender thing for it, and I know it is Ben's *cu* and this is why there is tenderness and why I feel my heart in my throat and I hope he can feel my heart, too.

I move him in my hand, the sweet softness of the flesh spilling between my fingers. He makes a sound. I tell my hand to be still. "Does this hurt you?" I say.

His face pulls away from my throat. He takes a deep and ragged breath. I do not want to stop touching him.

"I will hold my hand still," I say. "Please do not make me let go of you."

There is that little sound again, deep in his throat. I do not know if it means yes or no. But he says no words. I do not move my hand. My palm has grown as sensitive in its own way as the secret part of my own body, another part that I hesitate to name.

Her hand is on me and all day long I wandered the streets of Saigon, around and around, and I yearned for this moment and I dreaded this moment and my head is telling me now that it's okay, we've talked this out, it's come down to odds, that's all, one in twenty-five thousand, as easily ignored as the possibility I'd die each time I stepped into the cab of my truck in America and eased out onto the interstate. But I can't just go on like before. Her hand is on me and I should either touch her in return or I should tell her to stop and keep on trying to reason this out. But I can do neither thing, all I can do is say nothing and lie still and let her hand stay where it is.

But it's clear to me that my body won't respond. The part of me that's still out there in the street afraid to come up to this room and face what might be a terrible thing, is glad for that. The other part, the part that desperately wants a future in this woman's life, in her body, lifts my free hand and puts it on the top of her thigh. But can move it no farther. Tien and I lie there a long while like that. I am slack beneath her hand and my own hand is dead and distant.

Then she says, "Do you know what my sexual place there is called in Vietnamese?"

"No."

"It is âm-dạo. They are two words. Âm means secret. Dạo means path. It is my secret path. I think that is so, do you agree?"

"Yes," I say.

"But it is not a secret for you," she says. "To all others, yes. But not for you."

My hand moves at last, but not to this place on her. Instead to her face. I turn her face to me and I kiss her there. On the forehead. On her eyes, which she closes quickly for me, happily. One in twenty-five thousand. I want to kiss her mouth, too. This kiss on the forehead, as sweet and soft a place as this is on Tien, is a kiss that carries the shadow of that other thing. I want to open her mouth with mine and kiss her like the woman she is—she is a woman, she is no one's child—but I can't, I can't, her hand still clutches my penis softly and my kiss animates her there, she kneads me gently and I wish I could rise to her touch, I wish I could accept this secret she offers, but I am clenched there instead, from fear.

She says, "So this part of you must be a secret traveler then. Yes?"

Her voice is small and sweet and is talking around the edges of her desire for me. This pain now in me, a clear pain that has begun in my temples, will not let me answer.

She says, "Asleep at the edge of the forest. Resting for a while before pressing on."

I finally will these words. "You know I love you."

"I do?" She says it with the lift of a question in her voice.

"I want you, my sweet Tien. I want to be inside you very much."

"Oh please," she says with a rush. "I am not a girl who demands a man's body to do this or that when I say so. Please. I did not mean to criticize the sleepy one. I adore him."

She lets go of me and she sits up, my hand falling from her hip, my other coming from around her. She is straightening and now bending forward. She means to kiss me there, I realize. I cry out.

"Wait," I say. I slide up to sit before her. Her face is wide-eyed with shame. I grasp her hand. "Please don't

mistake me, now. You were about to do something
that . . ." Her hand is warm from touching me. I have
trouble saying what I know I must in order to reassure
her, not because it isn't true but because it is: I can see her
in my mind completing the gesture, leaning forward and
putting her lips on me there and she would kiss me with
the same delicate indirection of her voice and she would
be so utterly herself in that gesture and I want that very
badly and that is why I can't bear to have her do this, can't
bear to have even this image of her doing it, until who she
is and who I am are clear and certain.

"You don't like that?" she asks.

"I like it too much. Too much, my darling."

"You are still thinking the terrible thing."

"Yes." And admitting it, I suddenly let all the questions
back in. "The chances aren't one in twenty-five thousand,"
I say. "I found you here, didn't I?"

"This is where I live."

"Didn't you say this is the place where your mother left
you?"

"Yes."

"You lived here when she was working as a bargirl?"

"Yes."

"And where was her bar?"

"I don't know. She never took me there. Never."

"Near this place?"

"I don't know."

"You must know." I say this too loud. I can hear myself at once. She has flinched, drawn back a little. I reach to her. I take her hands in mine. "I'm sorry," I say.

She squeezes my hands. "Ben. It is my father causing this trouble."

I can't figure how to make sense of this.

"He is in this room," she says and I go cold, the place in my head that's been pounding goes sharp cold, mountain-pass cold.

She seems to understand. Her hands leap to my face, press at my cheeks. "No. No. I don't mean you. His ghost. My father is dead. Please believe that. His ghost is here trying to come between us."

I close my eyes. I'm still cold. I feel some asshole in me from Court TV boring on, filling my mouth with words when all I want in the world is just to do what Tien says, just believe her and go on with my life. I say, "I came to this street—you found me sitting downstairs—because this is where I knew the woman called Kim. This used to be a street full of bars. If your mother worked near here, then the chances turn into something really troubling."

No worse than that I'll have cancer growing in some part of me in the next twenty years, no worse chance than that, and I never think about that possibility: this is how I argue back. But I can't get warm again. I begin to shiver.

Tien leans forward and puts her arms around me. I say, "I have to know."

"How?"

I don't know for a moment. My mind thrashes its way toward obvious answers. "There are tests."

"You mean tests of the blood?"

"I think those are too broad. They won't tell us for sure. There are others."

"My darling, this is something I cannot say in my job, but we are in my bed naked, so I think it is okay. We do not have even enough medicine in Vietnam. We do not have enough doctors. We do not have laboratories for these things. I doubt we could even do the test of the blood. But surely not something more difficult."

I bow my head, close my eyes, focus on the stretching at the back of my neck. I think, How fragile these bodies are.

"There is one way," she says. She lifts at my face with her hand. I yield. Her eyes are very dark. The light is almost entirely gone from the room and the neon has not started up outside. She asks, "We must do this?"

I try once more to shake this thing off. I lift my hand. I touch her cheek. I think about kissing her mouth. Here in the gathering dark. The path is so secret that only she and I will know. Everyone I know in my life but her is an ocean away. All the Vietnamese on their motorbikes rushing past out in the street are ignorant of us, utterly ignorant. And if her father's ghost is in this room with us, then at least he isn't me. I bend to her. I bring my mouth to hers. Slowly. I feel her breath on my upper lip. Then we touch. Soft. And I hope she is right. And I think—part of me does, in this good moment, it thinks—she is right. But the very sweetness of this kiss makes me let it go and I pull back just out of the touch of her breath and I say, "Yes. I must know."

Do I even know myself how much I love this man? Until this moment I do not. I say, "I think my mother maybe has returned to her home village. It is near Nha Trang. We can try to find her."

He sits back. His face, though I cannot see it clearly now in the darkening room, seems suddenly blank. He does not want to do that any more than I do, I think. This makes me happy. Whoever this Kim might be, he does not want to see her again.

Though she is not my mother. She is not. This is something I still blame on my father's ghost. He puts all these confusing things inside Ben and me.

And then suddenly there is one more confusing thing. I have spoken of my mother's village to Ben without thinking, because it is true that she could easily have gone there, because if he must have some proof that is not in his own heart about this, then to find her is the only way. But I think now: Is she alive?

Sometimes in these past nineteen years I have wondered this. I did so when I served tea to Ben, his first time in this very room. But when I am thinking I will never know for sure, I will never see her again anyway, it is a distant idea. But now it comes to me very strong. She might be dead. And I argue with myself. She was not harmed by my government. I know that. None of the prostitutes for the Americans was harmed, not even here in Ho Chi Minh City, where some of them shamelessly remained and offered themselves to the liberation forces. These women simply were sent to be reeducated and none of them was harmed. And my mother would—I don't even know for sure how old she was when she left me; no more than thirty, I think—she would be perhaps fifty years old. No more. Perhaps still less. Not a woman ready to die of her years.

But she never came back. Even when it was clear—and it was quickly clear—that no harm would come to her, she never came back. She never even wrote a letter to my grandmother and me. She might be dead.

I feel a sudden chill. Not in me. In the room. I turn my face to look. There is nothing. The dark. The faceless shrine across the way.

"Do you think she might be there?" This is Ben's voice. He sounds very far away.

"Yes," I whisper and I listen for her. She might be in this room. It might be her jealousy, not my father's, causing this trouble.

"You haven't seen her since . . . ?"

I am hearing these words, I am even hearing the way he does not finish his sentence so that it becomes a question to me. But I am still straining to feel if she is in this room. I do not answer.

"Tien?" he says.

I turn to him.

He says, "If you don't want to do this, I understand."

"Do?"

"Find your mother."

"You have decided you need this thing?"

"I don't know. I want to just forget all this. I do. I want that more than anything. Just to touch you now."

He says this and I am watching his eyes. They do not move to my body, though I am still naked before him. And I know we must go to Nha Trang. The chill is inside me now. I am very conscious of my body. In the old way. I shrink before him even though he is looking only in my eyes. I fold my arms across my chest, hiding my nipples.

He says, "You haven't seen her since you were a child?"

"Eight years old," I say.

"Can you do this?"

"If it means we can love each other again. Yes."

"I love you now," he says.

"You know what I am saying."

"Yes," he says, and he looks away, toward the window.

I rise. His face suddenly turns pale red, as if he is blushing from the sight of me. But it is the neon that has come upon him like a ghost, from the outside, from the hotel across the street, lighting up for the night. Still, I find that I am hoping Ben will keep his eyes turned away from me until I cross the floor and disappear into the bathroom.

I turn my back to him and move away and my flesh crawls with the desire to be hidden. This makes me very sad. I try to feel if my mother is here with us. Before me, the bathroom door is ajar and the light from the bulb is spilling out. I stop. As much as I want to leave Ben's sight for now, I stop. I think it is her. I think I am her child again and she is there, behind the door, staying quiet, considering her spoiled life without my eyes upon her, perhaps staring into her own eyes in the mirror, like she did years ago, and she has come back now, to make trouble. I am afraid that all I have to do is touch the door and it will swing open and she will be there, her face turning to me.

But I am no longer her child. I am no one's child. If she is there, if her ghost has spun itself into something visible and is waiting for me, then I am happy for that. We will finish with this right here.

I step to the door and I open it fast. The bathroom is empty. My silk robe dangles on a hook on the back of the door. I take it down and I put it on. As soon as I do this, I feel better about my body, and as soon as I feel better about my body, I want to be naked again for Ben.

This is a very odd time for me.

But I draw the robe tight around me and I tie the belt and I do not like this bare bulb light. I step in and reach to it and I pull the chain. The darkness feels like a kiss on my eyes. I want it to be Ben's lips.

I come out of the bathroom and there is a shape in the dark, in the middle of the dark, and I fall back and it is large, filling the room, and I almost say aloud, Father, but the shape speaks, "What is it?" and it is Ben.

"I thought you were a ghost," I say.

He comes closer. I am glad now I did not speak. I wish I had left the light on. I want to see his face. I love his face. But the only light is the neon behind him and his face is dark and ringed in red, like the aura I have read that people give off, the living ghost we carry around. Though

I cannot see them, I could find his lips if I wanted to. But I know we must do this thing first.

I say, "You want to hire a Saigontourist guide for a road trip to Nha Trang. Yes?"

He does not say anything for a moment. I begin to hope that once we are away from this room, away from the spirits here, he might find the answer in himself, we might go to Nha Trang and simply swim together in the South China Sea without having to do more.

I say, "It has a very beautiful beach."

He says, "Can you arrange this tour?"

"Yes."

"Will it be . . . private?"

"My driver will be happy to have a secret holiday. Yes."

He is silent again. I am suddenly restless in my hands: they yearned to touch him tonight but they know it will not happen.

Then I say the thing that I want to feel but do not. "There is no reason to be afraid."

He says, "I can't tell you how sorry I am to put you through this."

I know what he means but I am not ready to think how it might be to find her. So I push the thought of this away from me, as I have done for all these years. I will simply let him be sorry for leaving my bed tonight.

"You will go to your hotel now?" I ask.

I hear him draw in a breath at this. It had not occurred to him yet. I grow a little impatient: it must be so, my Ben; you have led us to this; just accept it now and go. But I do not even come close to speaking these words aloud.

His shadow grows larger and he takes me in his arms and he lifts my face and kisses me on the lips, and though the kiss is brief, I feel if he lets go of me now, I will fall to the floor.

"When will I see you?" he asks.

"Tomorrow at noon in front of Ho Chi Minh," I say.

"The statue?"

"If you can find Uncle Ho himself, I will meet you there instead. He is very wise. Maybe his ghost can save us a trip."

Ben laughs softly and I laugh too, though I think I hear a little anger in me when I say that, but I am glad if he thinks only that I am a great kidder.

Then he is gone.

Outside her door I take a step and another and another and my legs are trying to throw me down and I lean against the balustrade on this long back balcony and I'm in front of somebody else's doorway, Tien's neighbor, and the door is open and a dim light is burning and there's a smell of kerosene and a wet, soupy smell—fish sauce and some cheap part of a pig—something like that, a food smell that's suddenly mixed up with an image of Kim, the smell in a back alley like this coming in through the window while I'm naked with Kim and it's been all these years and she's near me now and it could be in a room in this very alley, along this very common balcony, the place where I went in to make love for the first time. I press on. Another doorway standing open, a woman combing her hair out, long and dark, right now, not the past, I try to move faster, keep my eyes before me, and Kim is combing her hair before her dead grandfather's shrine and I am waiting naked on her bed.

I go down the twisting staircase, holding on tight, and I can see myself coming up metal stairs just like these, Kim climbing a step ahead of me, her sweet cheeks swaying in my face, making my hands itchy, the night smells of Saigon around us, wood fire, incense, alley rot. I'm moving away from Tien's rooms and all of this is coming back and I don't want to touch Kim, not even in my memory, I try to take the covers in this memory and pull them across my body as she combs her hair, but I can't, it's already happened, whatever it was between me and this woman whose name may not even have been Kim, it's happened and there's no taking it back and when I go there in my memory, as I'm doing now, trying to hurry along this alley, I can't cover myself, I remain naked and she crosses the room and I must pull her down to the bed with me, I must put my mouth on hers, I must feel her hand cup my penis, I must rise to her touch instantly.

I grab at my head with my hand, squeeze tight at my temples. She will go away for good when I know who she is. Or who she isn't. I'm out of the alley now and down the way is a pedicab and I move toward it and then I stop. I think that something here will tell me. I'll look closely and it'll be the wrong street altogether, the wrong part of town, the chances will turn long again. Another moment in a dark and distant night: I step down from a pedicab and I'm in front of a bar and I let myself be there, I try to see what it is in the window. Two Vietnamese words in neon, I think. Some of the bars had American names but not this one. This is the bar where she works and I can't remember the Vietnamese name for it. I look now and there's only the flickering fluorescence in the noodle restaurant, the tiny plastic tables in front ringed by the shapes of people eating. Was Kim's bar near the mouth of an alley like this? I try to look as I stand before the pedicab in my memory, but I can't see. The place floats in my head with nothing around and Kim is in the doorway, her face dark, the light from inside the bar ringing her head in gold. Was this the first moment I saw her? Hey GI, she says. Come in drink beer with Vietnam beauty, she says. My name Kim, she says.

I look around now. For something familiar, though I want there to be nothing. And there is nothing. Bodies move past me. Soup. Flats Fixed. A tailor's dummy in a window. It's all changed so much. The bars are long gone. The things that might still be the same—the alley, a balcony, a row of second-floor windows—are all a blur in my memory, or darkness. I turn around and looming over me is a big thing I should be able to remember: a hotel, the Metropole. But it's slick and clearly new. Or maybe remade. Was there a hotel across from Kim's bar? This feels faintly familiar. But I don't recognize this place. As big as this thing is, I can't say either that it was there or it wasn't. Something like panic revs in me, like the center of my chest is the engine for all these crazy feelings and it's revving into the red. I need to move. I need to get out of this street now, I think. But fuck that. I have to fight for Tien. If I can possibly find something that can end it here, something that will let me go back up to her now, right now, and say, It's over, we can be lovers forever, then I have to try.

I face the shop fronts. I let myself see the past. And there's nothing more. The street all around me is still black, like I'm passing out. There's only the bar in front of me. I stride across this space and I'm before the woman in the door and I say in my head, You're not Kim. That's for the GIs. What's your real name? She looks at me. I could have said those words at any time in those months I was with her. Just those few words and her answer—my real name is Kim—or any name at all except Huong—would put me in Tien's arms right now. But once we were more to each other than GI and bargirl, she could have told me her real name, if it was different, without my asking. She *would* have done that. Surely. And she never did. Isn't that as good? Isn't that proof? I want it to be all the proof I need, but it isn't.

So I turn away, I move to the pedicab and I speak the address of my hotel and we go off into the night. The motorbikes race past and I close my eyes and if the worst is true, then the last time I was with Kim, Tien was already there inside her body. I try to remember that and I find nothing. These things that remain—a moment on an iron stair, across a room, in the doorway of a bar—they're all snapshots—like a child under a tree, looking without a smile into the camera—they have no story to them, they tell me nothing. The thing between us just died. There was no revelation in the rush of our sex, there was no connection, there was nothing, and the cute words ended, I suppose, and there may have been money again, in the transaction, and then it was over for good. She wanted to come to America. A thing I couldn't give her. I said no. It ended like that. If she was pregnant, she would have used that to try to go with me. But she didn't. Unless she didn't know. But the way things were, it feels impossible that a new life had begun from what we'd done. I never went back to her. I never even went to another bar. I was dead to her and she was dead to me.

I shudder at this thought and I lean forward into the flow of the dark street beneath the pedicab. I went back to America alone and I married Mattie and I realized I was still alone and then I found my truck and the road, and on a run sometimes, I'd lean over my wheel and I'd watch the thin black track of exhaust burn on the highway as it rushed under me, and I felt it was leading me, sometimes I felt I was following this dark line into a future that held some big thing, like running after your fate instead of just driving another goddamn thousand miles one way to turn around and drive another thousand back again. There was more to me that I just hadn't reached yet. Much more.

Then I am lying in a bed on this night, in the dark, in my hotel in Saigon, and I wait for sleep and I wait for tomorrow. I know the road to Nha Trang, know it well: Highway One, where I watched the driver ahead of me, standing by the side of the road, part of him ripped away, and he was calm, very calm, wondering where that part might be. And there is the same stunned calm in me now, I think. I watch the paddle fan spinning above me and for the first time in my life, alone is not just the place I live in, sometimes with no one around, sometimes with a truck stop restaurant full of truckers, sometimes with a woman sleeping nearby in the bed. For the first time, alone means the absence of someone else: the crook of my arm, the point of my shoulder, the skin along my hip and thigh, all feel the prickle of her absent body, the shadow of her body still pressing there softly. I know the answer to the question that I share with the guy in the scrub grass by the side of Highway One. I know where the missing part of me is. She's in her own bed right now, in this very city. I was there tonight. And I walked out her door. Is she naked again? I am not. From fear of all this I am still in my clothes, afraid of my body now. But I can still feel her body on my skin. I'm sweating and the fan moves in the dark and I am alone.

When the door is shut, I cannot hold back my tears. For a few moments. But I stop them. I will not lose Ben. The room is dark. I go to the stand beside my bed and I turn on a lamp. The shade is thin and from the top comes light that is like the bulb in the bathroom. Is she here? Is she just out of my sight, keeping quiet? Someone knows the answer to that and I will talk to him now, as I have done every day of my adult life.

I cross to the shrine and I kneel and my hands go through the motions they know so well. I draw the box of

matches from beneath the skirt of the little table. I take
a match from the box and I strike it and the flame hisses
itself alive and I touch the tip of the first stalk of incense,
angling the match, putting the hot yellow point of the
flame on the blunt edge and it begins to glow and then the
incense seems to go dark, but smoke begins to rise and it
is burning, I know. I do this for the second stalk and the
third and I put the match flame before my lips and I blow
the flame away. I drop the match beside me. I press my
palms around the three sticks of incense and I pull them
from the sand. I bow my head.

Father, I say inside me. Father, I am here.

I lift the incense, help the smoke go up and into the
spirit world. I think of him turning his head. He smells
the scent of my prayers, carried from this fire with no
flame, and he moves from wherever it is that he goes in
that other world—I try to see the place but there is nothing, only darkness—and he comes to me now.

I say that I think of him turning my way, coming to
me, but I cannot picture his face. I have tried, often, in
my prayers, but whenever I see a face, I know very clearly
that it is only me, only my own construction from the
faces of other men: an Italian tourist, a Russian official,
Paul Newman. But though I cannot see him, he does
come to me here, my father. That much I do know, also

very clearly, and he is not a figment of my own mind, he is real.

Father, I say, I offer your spirit the peace that comes from the love and prayers and devotion of your child and I ask you for the harmony and the peace that a father can give to his family.

These are the words I always say, following the custom of the Vietnamese people. I am told that even some of our government officials pray to their ancestors. We are a communist country, caring for the masses according to the truths of Karl Marx, but we are also Vietnamese. I think perhaps the spirit of Karl Marx is wandering lonely and afraid in the afterlife because he and his children did not understand certain other truths. They were from Germany.

I place the stalks of incense in the sand once more and let the smoke rise on its own to carry the rest of my prayers.

Father, I say. You do not have to fear this man who loves me. I will not forget you. I say this to you, thinking again that it is you who has taken offense. Forgive me if I accuse you falsely, if it is my mother who is the jealous one. I ask you to let me know the truth. Is she there with you in the spirit world, causing this trouble between Ben and me?

I stop my own words and try to hear my father. He has spoken to me before, though not with the voice of a man. He puts his words into me whole and they grow there, from inside me. I wait for this to happen. My eyes are shut tight. There is only darkness. And the smell of incense. I am very still inside. And then I know he has told me. She is alive.

I open my eyes. I lift my face. Behind the three ribbons of smoke is the empty space where his face should be. I want to look him in the eyes so he can see my anger at him. But I have only words.

Father, I say, you must not try to make me choose. I am a living woman. Are you jealous of that, as well? You died a young man. Perhaps younger than I am now. But I have waited, Father. Until Ben touched me, no man had seen me naked in this room. Except you.

I pray these words and I stop. My face grows warm. I bow my head again but not in reverence. I am glad now not to look into his eyes. This thing that I had not thought of until today is very real inside me now, my being naked before him. And I have not told him of the two others, who saw me naked in other rooms.

I say to him, Why couldn't you be alive? Why couldn't you be alive and I could put the door between you and me and you could not see? And then I could dress myself and I could open the door and we could touch. You could take me in your arms. You could kiss my head. I could hold you close. I want that, too, Father. I ache for that too. But this man holds me in a different way. What we cannot have between us, you and me, is not replaced by what there is between Ben and me. I still yearn for you, Father. No less than before. See these tears streaming now from my eyes. They are for you. Not for the fear of losing Ben. For sadness at never touching you. Please take these doubts from Ben's mind now. Take them away. Call him your son and give him the peace that a spirit owes to the family he leaves behind.

I fall silent. I wait for his answer to this. But I sense nothing inside me. He is gone. He is in some other place, far away from me.

Ho Chi Minh's hand is on the head of the little girl. He's in black stone, and from seeing him the other day I remember his one arm outstretched on the tree stump where he sits and I remember his arm around the girl, who holds a flower. But I'm seeing this left hand now for the first time as I wait for Tien. His hand touches the little girl's hair and at first glance, it's a tender gesture, a paternal gesture. But I stare at this hand as I stand here waiting for Tien, with a rush of people around me and out in the street, and the hand is bothering me. It touches lightly, open-palmed, at the back and slightly to the side of her head, as if it is stroking her there, stroking her hair. A paternal gesture, too, I tell myself. But the girl seems so deeply absorbed by the flower in her hand, unaware of this touch, vulnerable in her ignorance, and Ho is not looking at her, his face is forward and there is a darkly adult look in his fixed eyes, his faintly ironic mouth. The sculptor wanted it both ways. Ho the gentle father figure and Ho the tough, focused leader of a revolution. But this look informs his hand and I fear for the little girl and I can't see this anymore and I find my own hands clenching, hard.

I turn away. A little girl slides past and she catches my eye and stops and she holds up a book of lottery tickets.

"You buy," she says.

"No," I say. "Sorry."

"You buy," she says, coming close. "Good luck win money."

"No," I say.

Her hand is on me, on my wrist. I yank the arm away.

"Go away. Please," I say.

"Fuck you," she says and she moves off and I rub at the place she touched, hard. Rub her touch away.

I jitter around. Move off from the statue. A man has a case opened up by a bench and it's full of packs of cigarettes. I draw near. I haven't smoked in years. I coughed my way one spring run from St. Louis to Denver and I stopped cold. But I want a cigarette now.

"You buy," he says.

I look at the brands, all Chinese or Vietnamese but all of them with names in English: Lord Filter. Ruby Queen. Park Lane. White Horse. Sunny. Hero. And there's a brand in a white pack called Memory. My hand goes out and it's trembling. I think Park Lane was the brand name that masked the marijuana when I was here. I pass it over, though I'm sure it's just tobacco now anyway. I take a pack of Ruby Queen and a pack of matches and I pay the man and walk away.

I open the pack and tap out a cigarette and put it in my mouth. I stuff the pack in my pants pocket and strike a match. I touch the end of the cigarette and pull the smoke in and it tastes like truck exhaust and I wait for the nicotine to kick in, to smooth out the rough spots, to steady my hand, but it only grates in me and all I'm getting is a shitload of blurry nights with a shitload of interstate exit signs drifting past in my headlights, and I flip the cigarette away.

I'm more jumpy than I was before. Then I see her crossing the street, far away, down at Le Loi near the fountain. I see her though there's a hundred people around her and a hundred people between us. I see Tien and she's dressed in that white blouse with the big bow and the dark, tight skirt that hides her knees. The way I first saw her.

She comes into the square and for a brief moment she doesn't see me. I think to walk away. As connected as I am to her by my love—and I am as connected to her as I am to the limbs of my body—I almost turn and walk away fast and find some place to hide and then get the hell out of this country without ever seeing her again and never ask another question of myself about what it was that happened. Go back and get into another truck and follow the black track of the exhaust burn in my lane till I fucking die. But I'm not quite scared enough to do that.

Then she sees me and she starts to hurry, cutting through the threads of Vietnamese strolling in the square, dodging people, and she doesn't seem to be one of them at all, she's moving in a different way, quicker, more focused. I think: Like an American.

And she is. Half of her is. That's already known. Watching her move like this, coming closer, is no reason for the revving to start again. I curse my cowardice. I curse these rushes of fear. I wait for her touch.

But it's not Saigon anymore, it's Ho Chi Minh City, and Ho is watching us and his own touch is secret, it seems to be one thing in this public place but is another, I'm certain now. Tien is here and she's breathing heavily and our hands flap out in front of us, not knowing what to do, and I don't quite know how it happens but our right hands connect and we shake, like two strangers meeting and introducing themselves, or maybe like tour guide and tourist. We both look down at our shaking hands and Tien laughs, though it is low, sharp, full, I think, of my failure last night.

"Hello," she says, still looking at our hands.

"Hello."

"This feels so strange," she says.

"Uncle Ho is watching," I say.

She brings her face up, glances over my shoulder. She laughs again, softer now, and then she says in a whisper, "He is easily offended."

"Good to meet you," I say, out loud, not letting go of her hand, playing the little game, though it's the last thing I want to do right now. "I'm Benjamin Cole."

"I am your guide, Miss Tien," she says, and she bends near. She whispers again. "Does this mean we can start over?"

I know she's asking if we really have to go to Nha Trang, if we can't just take another tour of the city and then meet tonight and resume our love affair. But I can't find a way to answer.

She says, "Out here. In this public place. Away from my room and all the . . . things that are in it. Does it seem the same to you?"

Our hands separate. I say, "I still love you."

"And I love you. But it is the other thing I ask about. The fear."

I wait. I wait for some other answer than the one I know I must give. But there is nothing else. "We have to know for sure."

She nods once. "Then I have reserved a car for us. I wish it was right now. But the soonest I could arrange was in three days' time."

"Three days." It's dumb repetition. I don't know how to hold this feeling for three extra days.

"I'm sorry," she says. "The city is full of Japanese businessmen until the weekend. They have booked many weeks in advance."

"I understand."

There are no words for a long moment and then she says, very softly, "Until then, it must only be a handshake for us. Is that not so?"

I look closely at her eyes. Surely if she is my daughter, I'd be able to look in her eyes and see something of myself and know. But there is nothing clear. And the fear won't go away.

Tien nods as if I've answered her. She says, "I will see you on Friday. I will meet you with the car just over there, in front of the Rex Hotel, at eight in the morning. We can get very close to Nha Trang before the night."

I say, "Are you angry with me?"

"No," she says. "Not with you. I am angry with my father."

What races in me now is gratitude for this woman. Her certainty lifts me, smooths the rough spots like I'd expected from the hit on the cigarette. I say, "I want to touch you now more than ever. You understand?"

"I wish not to understand until it can be more than words."

"I love you, Tien."

Her eyes fill with tears, but she lifts her chin slightly, keeps them from flowing. She offers her hand. "I will shake your hand for that," she says.

I smile. She does too. I take her hand as if to shake but our hands do not move. We touch and people pass by, close to us. She releases my hand and goes off, past me.

I do not turn to watch her and suddenly she is near me again, at my side.

She says, "I do not want you to misunderstand for these three clays. When I shake your hand just now, I was full of some strong feeling about you, a good feeling. I did not say in return 'I love you,' but I do."

And she's gone. I watch her this time as she moves off, past Ho with his hand on the child, and into the crowd. When I lose sight of her, I dig my own restless hands into my pockets and I find the pack of Ruby Queens. I tap out

another cigarette and I light it up and I suck in a deep drag
and it burns in me but I keep it in and all the empty nights
on the road come with it, all the nights pulling smoke in
and letting it out, over and over, and I keep the smoke
inside me now, like holding my own ghost.

He is on the curb when Mr. Thu and I drive up. He has a
small bag beside him and we stop. I can see his forehead
wrinkle when he sees Mr. Thu. I get out. We do not shake
hands this time.

"You remember Mr. Thu," I say, even before he can
ask. "We will drop him at his house on our way out of
town."

Ben nods. I open the back door for him. Mr. Thu is
already out of the car and picking up Ben's bag and he
heads for the trunk. "Please," I say to Ben, motioning him
into the backseat. I feel how formal I am, how distant this
all sounds. He does too. He gives me a brief, sad look and
he moves and bends, entering the backseat. I do not care if
anyone sees or what they think, though I am very discreet,
really, turning my body to shield this thing I do, but as he
goes by me I move the hand holding the door and touch
him on the back of his thigh, just a quick touch and I grasp
the door again and close it.

I step away from the car and my heart is racing. I should be more considerate of Ben's fear. But I will not share it. I am looking for this trip to escape my father, not find my mother. I will not even think of my mother. Somewhere along Highway One, well before Nha Trang, I think things will become clear on their own.

I turn from the car. I look around. The xich lo drivers are in a clump in the midst of their cabs, arguing about something. The doorman at the Rex is looking down the street. No one has seen my counterrevolutionary act. I get into the front passenger seat. As soon as I close my door, I hear the trunk slam shut. I look into the backseat at Ben. I want him to be smiling, happy for my touch. He is not. His eyes are very sad.

I say, "I am sorry."

"Why?"

"For touching you."

Mr. Thu is opening the driver door, unaware what we are saying in English.

"Don't you know what it is I'm afraid of?" Ben says.

"Of course I know."

The door closes. Mr. Thu is beside me.

Ben leans forward and touches my shoulder, just with the tips of his fingers, and he sits back deep in his seat again, his eyes looking out the side window. I tell Mr. Thu to take us to his house.

Mr. Thu lives in a place where I have taken many foreign officials and businessmen, a New Economic District where the rapid development of the Socialist Republic of Vietnam is very clear. There are many streets, soon to be full of children and trees, where blocks of beautiful apartments, constructed from highest grade portland cement made in modern factories in Can Tho, glisten white in the sunlight. We drive down such a street and stop. Before Mr. Thu gets out, he and I speak a little in Vietnamese— he thanks me for this time off, because he has a sick child and his wife's two brothers and their families are visiting from Hanoi, and I thank him for letting me take the car—and while I am speaking my own native language, I am feeling very strange. I am thinking very much how Ben cannot understand what I say or what I hear. And I am hearing even the English in my head as a foreign thing, words about cement production and economic development. And I know I cannot touch Ben when Mr. Thu is gone, though that is what my body yearns to do. This strange feeling makes itself clear to me: I feel suddenly like a person who does not know who she is.

Then Mr. Thu is out of the car and walking away and I watch him until he has disappeared into one of these modern socialist-state apartments. I sit for a moment even after he has gone and I do not say anything and I do not look into the backseat. Ben is silent, too. I am the ghost now. I think what it must be like for my father, watching someone he loves without a language to speak with or a body to touch with.

Then Ben speaks my name. "Tien."

I turn. He slides forward in the seat. Our faces are very near. I wait but this is as close as we are going to get. So I ask him, "Are you ready?"

"Yes."

"Do you think you can drive on Vietnam's roads?"

"You forget what I used to do here."

"My truck driver."

"I know the rules. Never stop. Small gives way to large."

"You are ready to be as dangerous as my countrymen."

He smiles at this thing I say. I am glad. He gets out of the car and goes around and he slides in behind the wheel, beside me.

I clutch the steering wheel and it's a stunningly familiar thing. To drive and not to feel.

"What have you done these three days?" This is Tien's voice and I turn to her, trying to hear what it is that she's said.

Finally I answer, "I've watched a paddle fan spin on the ceiling."

"I have no fan to watch. I have only tourists and prayers to a man I think maybe does not hear me anymore."

My hands are cranking the engine. I want to drive now.

Even though it's not a truck and an interstate. It's a Fiat sedan with a Saigontourist sticker across the back windshield and an alien street rimmed by an ugly block of apartments. And another street, running through a cleared field waiting for more concrete, and another, packed full with motorbikes squeezing past ramshackle produce stands and restaurants and warrens of scrap wood and corrugated-sheet-metal houses. She tells me where to turn, but says no more than that. I'm glad. I want to hold a wheel and drive in the silence that was my life for years. Even going slow. Even with young men with black flares of hair and young women in sunglasses looking in on all sides while I creep ahead only to find myself in another press of new eyes. It's all right. I'm holding the wheel, I'm moving, I turn off the air-conditioning and roll the window down and let in the smell of exhaust, a smell of the road, and I have a place to drive to, a place ahead that will resolve all this.

And finally the city traffic loosens somewhat and the road widens a little and though it's full of potholes and oxcarts and trucks pushing in front of me or jumping out of the oncoming lane and forcing me over, still I can push a bit and I lay on my horn and the women on bikes and the tiny three-wheel Lambretta buses and all the motorbikes give way for me. I just stay clear of the trucks and they're funky-ass things, for the most part, old deuce-and-a-halfs or old commercial De Sotos and Jimmys, with jerry-built water tanks on the tops of their cabs and copper tubing feeding down into the engines, doing the work of long-gone radiators that can't be replaced.

And then we're farther out of town, heading for where Long Binh must've been, a massive Army base camp out northeast of Saigon, the place we all passed through on the way into the war. And there are billboards: an enormous display of a piece of PVC pipe, a giant tube of some Hong Kong toothpaste, and a billboard that pleads, GOLF VIETNAM. And then there's a turnoff to the place where a sign says they're building the Vietnam International Golf Club. I try to figure how far we've come, to see if they're building that right there on the doorstep we used for all the guys to come and fight in Vietnam. But I don't think the government that has filled Tien with all those little riffs of ideology would have the sense of humor for that.

I think of her. I look. She has her face turned to the rush of countryside. A flooded rice paddy now. Women out there in conical straw hats bent into their work, up to their ankles among the low green plants. And a boy near

the road on the back of a water buffalo. I look to the highway and I swerve around a pothole as big as the buffalo's
head.

But being on the road is good. The road rolls, even
if you've got to dodge and honk and give way. Your life
passes. You get through the hours you wouldn't know how
to get through if you were sitting still somewhere. And I
must have missed whatever was left of Long Binh because
we're going through a town called Honai and there was
nothing like that between Saigon and the camp. We're
crawling again, but still moving. Four Catholic churches
almost one after the other. And no pictures of Ho out
here. It's a country I don't expect.

Then the road again and rubber trees, a plantation, the
quick run of the even, deep rows of trees, their white
trunks all with the same dark slashes, and a grave out
there, a little stone monument in the trees. I follow it
with my eyes and I see Tien again and she's looking, too,
turning to see the tomb. I think to speak to her. At least
to explain my silence, though surely it's best for her, as
well. It's a kind of touching, our talk. This trip is hard
on her and I'm very sorry for that. But the rubber trees
vanish and now there's a pond, and I turn to the road and
it is narrowing down, and something is fitting together in
my head and Tien slides away from me once more. The
pond—I look again before it's gone—the pond curves

away from the highway and out to the north and it's shaped like a sickle blade and the sun flares there and is gone and the pond is gone and I know the place. Ahead, the road has narrowed but tree lines have taken up, maybe a hundred yards back, on both sides.

And suddenly this feels like the place. I have never remembered these things—the rubber trees, the curving blade of a pond, the narrowing of Highway One—even in my dreams of that day. But now it's clear. I slow down, I draw off the road, the shoulder is narrow, but I squeeze far over, the wheel bucking a little in the uneven ground, and I stop.

"What is it?" Tien says.

I get out of the car. A truck flashes past, ragged and Army green, and its horn blares and Dopplers away down the road. I look and it's full of hay but it's still a deuce-and-a-half, a truck from some old convoy, and I know where I am, I feel sure I know, and a cluster of motorbikes races by, a voice floating out, shouting, meaningless words. I start across the road. Hurrying before another truck coming from the north. And I'm off the road and the truck's draft buffets me and I wade into the scrub growth and I stop and he could have stood right here.

I turn. I stand just as he stood, the blond guy with the missing arm. I wait. The sounds from the highway are faint now. I wait for something to clarify itself. I try to see him again. It's been a year or more since I've dreamed about him. But when I did, he was very clear. And two years before that, clear. But he's dim now. How odd, to find this place because of new memories, restored memories—the pond, the plantation—but now that I'm in the place again, the man who made all these memories important has faded. I can't see his face anymore, it's all darkness, as he looks at what's happened to him. He's an outline, blurred by the sun.

I lift my hands. I stare at them before me. My two hands. And then I look across the road. Tien's face floats there in the window of the car. She has slid across to the driver's seat so she can see what it is I'm doing out here without a word of explanation to her, and her eyes are clear from this place where I stand, dark and steady on me, and I feel her on the palms of these hands. I am in Vietnam, the place where I went to war for my father. I saw an image here, in this very field, an image that clung to me not by its horror or its strangeness but by how it fit all that I had felt till then and all that I would feel for years after. And it's gone now. Gone. And in its place is this image across the road. The face of this Vietnamese woman, watching me, waiting for me, she has opened her body to me, and in it, this other image dissolved. A great dark mass erases her face, the flash of a truck, and for that moment he's there again, like the flare from the first rocket in the attack, his face calm except for the knot of puzzlement in his brow, and the truck is gone and it's Tien instead. Puzzled, too, I know.

I move through the scrub, onto the shoulder, I look and a Lambretta is coming and a motorcycle and to the right is a provincial bus, bright yellow and green and people are clinging to the doors and hanging out the windows and my legs don't stop, I can't wait to cross to Tien, horns cry from both directions and I rush now, hard, I feel the wisp of a flap of a woman's ao dai across my back from the motorcycle and the grille of the bus bloats near me I feel it on my face and I lunge and it goes by trailing voices and I stumble in the uneven earth and I fall, palms and knees going numb and then my chest in the brush.

She is beside me. Her hands on my face, on my back, my arms, touching and moving, and her voice is with them. "Are you all right, my Ben? What is it, my love?"

I'm sitting now, brushing at my chest, and she takes my face in her hands, her touches are like kisses, like we're kissing, and for the moment it's okay, for the moment there's nothing of my fear, only this release of the boy in the field, only Tien's hands on me. I take one of them and turn it and I kiss the palm.

"Oh my," she says.

"I'm sorry," I say.

"What was that about?"

"The kiss?"

"I hope I know what that was about. The other."

"I remembered something."

"You remembered to run in front of a bus?" She pinches both my cheeks at this, like a mother scolding a child. I am surprised at the comfort I feel from this gesture.

Her hands retreat. I look into her eyes. They are steady, soft with what I know is her love for me.

I say, "I left you without a word. I wanted to explain."

"You would have much to explain if you died there. I would interrogate you very sharply, Benjamin Cole."

"Do that again," I say.

"What?"

"Pinch my cheeks when you scold me."

She cocks her head at me, smiles that half-smile which was my first vision of her.

She lifts her hands, twists at my cheeks, though the comfort of this is gone now. She says, "My father is jealous enough as it is. Imagine if he had to share my shrine with you."

I lift my own hands, cover hers. She flattens her palms against my face. We stay like that until a motorcycle brats past and voices cry out at us. She does not show even a flicker of recognition at the words, but she says, "This is a public place, my Ben. And this is not part of our tour package, these caresses."

Our hands fall. I climb to my feet. I look once more across the road. The place is bland, a ragged field, distant trees.

I feel her draw near me. "Ben," she says softly.

"Yes?"

"Should we go on? Or go back to a private place?"

I look at her. For a moment all that had been set aside. And even now the desperateness is gone. But when she asks the question, something of the darker question remains. "Did you tell me Nha Trang has a lovely beach?" I ask.

"Yes," she says. "There are private places on the South China Sea."

"We'll go there. Maybe just for the beach."

She does not speak, but I hear a sound from her, a soft thing, a flow of her breath that I wish was on my naked chest.

We move to the car and when we are inside, seated side by side, and my hand is about to move to the keys in the ignition, she says, "So what was it you rushed into the traffic to explain?"

I have no words for a time. I wait. I squeeze at the steering wheel and wait. Finally I say, "The past. I'm trying to let go."

"This is very good," she says. And her hand steals across the seat and touches my thigh and then retreats again.

It is not clear to me what we are to do after Ben tries to let go of some part of his past there on the side of the road. It is not clear to him either, I think. So I try to make myself slow down. I feel very much like a new socialist woman, an equal worker in the new social order, which means to me you can touch your husband when you want to and you do not have to wait for him to decide this. But I must consider his feelings, too.

I have thought *husband*. I cannot stop a smile at this word. I am telling myself how I should slow down, and even in the telling, I am going very fast. I watch out the window and I think that in Nha Trang, by the sea, in the wind off the South China Sea, all the spirits of the past will be blown far away and Ben and I can find a place alone together.

For now, I keep my hands in my lap and my eyes out the window. Perhaps I doze. I have not slept well for these three nights and my eyes grow heavy. Along the side of the highway women have spread out rice to dry and then it is manioc root drying there, the white chips they use for flour, and then it is coffee and now I know for sure I have

slept, for we are passing the Long Khanh mountains, past
Xuan Loc, a town which I have missed, which was a bat-
tlefield where our nationalist forces had many victories,
and on the side of the road the dark brown beans are laid
out to dry and the smell of the coffee fills the air.

I turn my face to Ben. I watch him for a while without
him knowing. He is very intent on the road. His hands on
the wheel are large, my truck driver's hands, which know
my body, which are part of my own body. There are shadows flashing over us. I look outside and we are running
beneath eucalyptus trees, lining both sides of the highway,
their bodies white, their thin arms drooping like mothers
mourning, and beneath them some little girls in white ao
dais are riding bicycles. Ben is driving slow now among
these children.

It leads me to speak whatever I can find to say, just to
touch him with my voice. "These are eucalyptus trees,"
I say. "An oil comes from this tree that we use when we
are sick."

He does not seem to hear me at first. I watch ahead and
we pass the last of the girls on bicycles and then an oxcart
and we are free also of the trees and I do not expect any
words in return now, but he says, "There are eucalyptus in
California, along the highways to break the wind."

These words make me as happy as if he has suddenly
kissed me. But still, I can hear his voice working hard in

order to speak. I watch a spot in the sky, out ahead of us, near a grove of cashew trees. It seems to be a great bird hovering, hanging motionless against the sky. We near, and the bird moves to one side and then jerks back to the other, and I know it is a kite. There is a child, invisible to us, beyond the trees.

"Tien," Ben says, low. "I'm sorry if I'm quiet. I've driven half my life, nearly, and it has always been in silence."

"I understand," I say.

We pass the cashew trees by. The sky is empty now. I take this explanation as an act of love.

He says, "There's a quiet place in me, since I stopped by the road. I want to keep that. I want it when we reach the sea."

"Yes," I say. "It is a good thing, this silent time." I struggle with my hands, to keep them where they are, in my lap. They obey this time. I try to find that quiet place in me now, too.

And so, together, Ben and I become the landscape rushing past us. Red soil and the smoke of brick kilns and piles of brick along the road, and roof tiles. And in Phan Thiet, TV antennas on bamboo poles and in the air the smell of nuoc mam, our wonderful fish sauce that they make in the town, and then, beyond, the salt flats with their little levees of tan mud and great squares of seawater and the piles of white salt taller than a man, and then paddies again and the smell in the air of rice hay burning and swarms of ducks grazing the wet fields after the harvest, and then coconut trees and then the Truong Son mountains to the west. And the mountains slide over and squeeze us next to the sea. And the sea is there for Ben's eyes, our first sight of it together, the South China Sea, sudden and vast coming out from behind the dunes and bright from the sun, and it is the dark green of the finest jade.

And now I steal a look at Ben, and his face is turned my way, though his eyes are far out to sea already. He glances at me and out again and then to the road. "We'll lose it again for a few hours, won't we," he says, and I know he means the sea.

"Yes," I say.

And we go on. And we stop only briefly at a roadside stand to eat, and we sit on tiny plastic chairs in the shade of an umbrella and I keep my eyes away from Ben, because his knees are almost up to his ears as he sits on this thing meant for a Vietnamese, and I like the size of him and I like him looking funny and not even realizing it, but these are the kinds of things I must put aside for now. Still, I am beginning to thrill again, like on the afternoon when I was preparing to make love to him, though we did not make love on that day, the preparation was a very sweet thing, and now I am having the same feeling. We are going fast. We will be at the sea near Nha Trang before the sun is gone.

So we go back on the road and soon we are passing tobacco drying in racks, the large green leaves, like the ears of elephants, and somewhere I think they must be burning the scrap because there is a strong tobacco smell suddenly around us and Ben is moving beside me. I look and he has lifted a little in his seat to dig in his pocket, and he pulls out a pack of cigarettes. This is a surprise for me. I have never seen him smoke. He does not take his eyes off the road. He does not take out a cigarette. He holds the pack for a moment, as if thinking about it, and then he tosses it into the backseat.

And what can it be that whispers in my body at this moment? I am a practical woman, a good citizen of a serious Marxist state, and this part of me says it is the food I ate by the side of the road, upsetting my body, just that, and perhaps also the smell of tobacco, which makes me feel a little bit unbalanced, since I have never smoked a cigarette in my life. Even perhaps it is some idle idea, a public health issue, since the man I love—the man who I am believing, in some shuttered-up room in my mind, will be living with me forever —has just rejected the smoking of a cigarette. I know that the smoke from a cigarette can harm others, especially delicate others. All

of these things may be what turn my face to the landscape and whisper such an important message to me, so
important that as soon as the thought comes, I ignore
the message itself and instead I start thinking around and
around about how it might have been prompted by nothing but indigestion or some other trivial thing. And even
knowing how it is that I am avoiding the thought itself,
I go on trying to discredit it. It could be a trick of the
mind: I have just seen a Cham woman walking ahead of
us and we raced past her and I turned to see her and she
was carrying a baby in a pouch on her chest. The Cham
are from different ancestors than other Vietnamese. They
are Hindus. They have a god called Shiva who is very
powerful and very terrifying to look at and who waits to
destroy the world, and I can certainly understand Karl
Marx being uncomfortable with religion when I hear
of this god, I do not want to believe in this god either.
Maybe this woman and her god and her baby are what
make me feel this thing about my body.

And how can the most important message of my life be
whispered to me in a moment like this? But it can. It can.
For though I am in a Saigontourist car and I am watching
two ragged dogs running beside us barking at the edge of
this village and though my stomach is a little queasy from
the soup I had by the side of the road and my head is a
little light from the smell of tobacco, it was five days ago

that Ben and I made love and I told him to stay inside me and now suddenly there is something deeper in my body I clearly can feel, something, like a shifting in my bones, like a quickening in my blood, something.

But I am a clearheaded modern woman. I know things about a woman's body. And so I count the days, a thing I have not thought to do until this moment. And from that night to my next bleeding, it is two weeks.

I sit with this for a while.

There is no thought in my head.

But there is a deep shadow all around me, a secret place inside a banyan tree where I am a child myself and I have my first most vivid thought of a woman giving birth: a princess laying one hundred eggs. I know that Ben is nearby—I feel him next to me; he is enormous there—but the world he fills is just outside the root-trunk of this tree where I am, where I listen to the tale of the dragon and the princess, and it is Tien the child who listens, but I am there, too, Tien the adult, and I am inside the child, waiting to be born from her. And we are Chinese boxes, the tree and Tien the child and me. And my baby.

I try to return now, to the car. I lean into the rush of air through the window, I squint into the bright after-noon, the air full of the smell of wood fires, some village out of sight. I close my eyes. I lay my hands on my belly and Ben is nearby. I could reach out my hand and touch him, but I do not even look at him for now. His presence makes me very happy but it also fills me with terror, for there are questions I do not even begin to let inside my head, even simple questions about where I will live for the rest of my life, in what country, questions that I cast away from me, including the question of what to say to Ben. Nothing. For now, nothing. I do not drift again to the banyan tree, but I do think of the fairy princess once more. How she took inside her the seed of a dragon, and how she must have wondered what child would come of this.

The road goes on and though there's no white line and no flat-out running, it does me some real good. Things are clean in my head out here, with an engine in front of me and a place to go to. And Tien is still beside me. She hasn't disappeared in order for me to feel like this. And that's the best thing of all. I don't have to go back to being alone to make things simple. Tien loves me. I love her. We're on the road together. The night is coming. It's boiled sweetly down to that.

Still, I don't turn us back to Saigon. I don't want to give up the wheel. Out here on Highway One, I'll go to sleep and wake up tomorrow morning with more miles to drive. Back in Saigon, it's just the paddle fan or that room of Tien's, which she thinks was part of my little scare, and maybe it was. Wherever it came from and however nasty it was, that panic was actually worth it, it seems to me now, to get Tien and me on the road together. Driving has been the way out for me for so long that being able to bring Tien into it was a necessary thing for the two of us to go on from here.

I'm glad my mama made me read all those books. I think I picked a few things up, hearing all those voices. But they didn't do me jack shit when it came to the minute-to-minute drag of that life back there. I told Tien the truck driving didn't solve anything either, and it didn't, in the long run. That's true. That's why her sitting here next to me now as we go up Highway One is so important. But there was a place I'd get to inside me, sometimes, driving the highways, when the silence would feel comfortable, when being alone was a natural thing, and it was usually at night and I'd be watching the lane break in my headlights and it turned into a kind of white-line mantra and there'd just be this soft ticking in my head, with those white lines going by, and things would be okay. And then I'd hit a truck stop and I'd go in and some old woman would be dozing behind the register and maybe one or two other guys were hunched over some coffee and I'd rent a shower stall and go on back along some white-lit hallway and unlock a door and hang the key on the hook and I'd strip down and run the water and the grit of the road would roll off me and the water would feel almost as sweet and good as a shower in Vietnam, where you thought something as simple as that, a goddamn shower, could never ever feel as good again in your life. But once in a while it almost did, out on the highway.

And the sun is getting low and there's just salt flats and shrimp ponds going by on the east side of the road. The South China Sea hasn't reappeared. I turn to Tien. Though I've been conscious of her there, and happy for that, I haven't looked directly at her for a long while. She has her hands tented in front of her, palms together, her chin resting on the tips of her middle fingers. Her eyes are closed. There's a faint smile on her face. She could be sleeping or praying or playing beautiful music in her head, something very private. I look back to the road and keep my mouth shut.

But somehow she knows. She says, "Do you wish to stop?"

I look to her again. Her hands have settled in her lap. Her faint smile has turned to me. I say, "Nha Trang isn't far, is it?"

"Less than an hour. Do you want to stay in the city?"

"Isn't there a more private place, by the sea?"

"We can go east up ahead. There's a narrow road to the shore."

"What's there?"

"A villa once owned by . . . I was going to say a member of the puppet government of the south. I have caught myself. Am I not a changed woman?"

"Yes. And I'm a changed man." I lay my hand, palm up, on the seat between us and her palm settles on mine and her fingers close softly and it feels like sex, for the first time in days our bodies are really touching and it runs through me fast and I punch the accelerator.

Up the highway, she motions and we turn off, and the narrow road is made of packed dirt and it's rutted and it's slow going, and then, at last, I can smell the salt water, and we go over a little rise and the South China Sea is before me, darkening now at the end of the day.

"Over there," she says, and off to the right is a large, rambling house facing the sea, and I turn into a shell drive rimmed with palms and I slide up to the front walk and stop. Tien says to wait and she gets out of the car and I turn off the engine. There's still the crawl of the road in my head and the vibration of the engine in my arms but there's a letting go, too. My shoulders sag and the car ticks and I can hear the sea on the other side of the villa. I lay my forearm on the steering wheel and my forehead against my arm and I wait, feeling the cloak of the road on me, wanting to take that off. I'm ready to be naked with her again.

Then she's at my window, leaning near. "Leave the car here," she says. "We have a room."

I should rent two rooms for us, for the appearance of it, but I tell the woman who runs the guesthouse we are married, we are Mr. and Mrs. Benjamin Cole, and I believe it is true, in a way. I am not sure if the woman believes me, but I do not care. I so much want Ben to sleep in my arms tonight.

Ben and I walk around the house and beneath a gallery and suddenly the sea stretches wide before us. To the north, the beach curves toward Nha Trang, which is invisible beyond the big shoulders of some hills at a distant turning. No one is on the shore. Out in the sea is a little string of four fishing boats, heading back to Nha Trang. Their engines beat faintly over the rushing sound of the waves. I have just begun to listen to this sound, which is a familiar thing, when Ben says, "It's like the motorcycles in Saigon."

I look at him. He is reading my mind now, not even my mind, he reads my ears. "They'll be gone soon," I say.

He looks to the south and I do too. Perhaps half a kilo-
meter or more away, there is some figure on the beach, but
that is not clear. Otherwise there is no one. The land along
the sea flattens out and stretches far away. Ben takes in a
slow breath of this sweet air. Now I try to name his thought.

I say, "We are alone on this sea."

"Yes," he says. "It feels that way."

I was right about what was in him. I smile. "There is no
one staying at this place tonight but us. The tourists who
come along here go on to Nha Trang, I think."

He turns to me abruptly. "Come on then. There's still
some light."

He drops his bag on the ground and holds out his hand.
I lift my own hand and I move it toward his and even
before we touch, it feels as if I have a shadow body inside
this one that he can see, and my hand nears his and the
body inside, which normally fits snug inside me, has loos-
ened for him and then the tips of our fingers touch and
I begin to quake inside my skin. His hand grasps mine
firmly and we are moving across a grassy plot and onto
the beach, the sand gray and packed hard, and he lets go
of my hand and he pulls off his shoes and drops them. I
pull off my shoes too, knowing I will destroy my stockings, thinking to ask him to go back to the villa and into
our room beneath the gallery facing the sea, for only a
brief time, so I can change from these tour guide clothes.

But he is groping for my hand again with an eagerness that makes me feel like we are two children and I am angry with myself, thinking of my stockings.

He moves quickly now, almost running, and I run with him and all I am thinking is my stockings should go to hell, my life has changed, and now all that I regret about my clothes is that I have not stripped them from me.

We are at the waterline, the waves bubbling and swiping at us, and we turn to the north, where there is not even a hint of a distant figure, and we move together by the South China Sea and the water splashes up our ankles and I say, "Wait."

We stop, and again I look ahead, and behind, and even the speck that might have been a person to the south is gone, and to the west there are only dunes and rocks and the creep of the mountains toward the sea. We are alone. So I lift my skirt, and I find the rim of my panty hose with my thumbs, and I grasp only the hose and not my panties underneath, and I strip them down and roll them soggy and ragged off one foot and then the other and my thighs and my legs and my ankles and my feet are naked, and I throw the panty hose into the sea—let some crab inhabit them—and I let my skirt back down to where it was. I look and Ben has squared around to watch this. He lifts his eyes to mine and he smiles and then I gasp as he falls forward and he is on his knees before me and he lifts my skirt again and he bends and I feel his lips on one knee and then on the other and I lift my face to the hunch of the distant mountains and my skirt climbs and he kisses one thigh and then the other. My hands fall to the top of his head, but lightly, so as not to discourage him. I wish now I had stripped off the panties as well. I do feel a pressure there, on that most tender of spots on my body, his mouth is there, but I do not feel the flesh of his lips on me. I lift my hands from his head, ready to take this barrier from between us, but he rises and his arms are around me and I am in his arms and his mouth is on my mouth, briefly, and then he has turned again, taken my hand again, and a great surge of the sea bumps us, rises quick up my leg, floats my hem, jealous, I think, of Ben's kiss, wishing to kiss me there, too, and we try to stay on our feet, from the nudging of the sea, and Ben laughs and lets go of my hand and moves on ahead.

I know I am to follow, but this sudden vision of him, his whole body at once, moving, is a rare thing for me. I have seen him very close up far more often. The sea runs away from me, too, and I move after Ben, but slowly, angling up the beach a bit, letting him go. He loves the water. I can feel this in him. He is twenty or thirty meters ahead of me now, slowing, watching out to sea. The fishing boats are tiny, about to disappear, the sound of their motors has dwindled into silence.

And now his shirt is off, flying back behind him up the beach. And he is stripping his pants down and my breath catches, I think to do this too, throw off my clothes and run to him, but I am still loving to watch, and he strips off his underpants and my Ben is naked and his shoulders are broad like the hills at the turn of the beach and his back is straight and his bottom is small and my hands stir, this is a part of him I have not seen yet, really, and I want to lay my palms on this sweet part of him, and he is striding forward now into the water.

He has not looked back to me. He is thigh deep in the water and now his bottom has disappeared and he is pushing hard and he still has not looked over his shoulder—it is like he has forgotten me—and something dark comes into me, an old thing, and he falls forward and I see the flash of his arms and his legs and he is lifted by a wave that does not break and he falls and he is still swimming and I know what the dark thing is, it is the dragon, how he missed his kingdom in the sea and one day simply was gone. The princess—who was his wife and the mother of his children—woke and he had gone back to the sea.

I want to cry out to Ben. I take a step forward. He is far out now—how quickly he seems to have gone—he rises on a distant swell and the swell falls and I do not see him. He has vanished. I cry out at last, a pitiful sound, a tight pathetic sound that no one can hear, and I am rooted where I am, I cannot move and I am clothed tight and I am suddenly alone. I keep my eyes fixed there, where he was a moment ago. I wait. I wait. The sea swells again and falls and there is foam and breakers and there is a vast sky, going dark, going very dark, and still Ben does not reappear. He is gone. I touch my belly. I press there. I do not want our child to follow him.

Then his head—far away—appears in the sea. He shakes his head sharply, clearing water from his face and now I can see him looking to the shore, he is looking for me. I lift my arm, I wave, and his arm comes up from beneath the water and he waves, and then he disappears again. But before the darkness can clutch at me once more, his body comes up and he is swimming, fast, lifting with a swell and speeding in and then dropping, but I can see him instantly again, and he swims and rises and falls, over and over, and now he angles upright and he is wading toward me, the water to his chest and then to his waist.

I am quaking again, for it is time. I have not looked at this part of him yet and now it is time. He moves, the water falls, a dark splash of hair appears, but the water swells, up to his chest, pushing him to me, and then suddenly the sea dips and I can see him there. Not nearly so large as it felt inside me, this part is withdrawn into the circle of the rest of him there, like a cameo, but he is

coming from the sea and I know he will grow with my
touch. He is striding now from the foam of the breakers
and I keep my eyes on this part of him and he quakes there
like this quaking inside me and he is drawing nearer and
even as I am watching him, this part is changing, growing, from the touch of my eyes, no longer a cameo but a
clasp now, a great clasp to connect to me and to hold me
tight and to carry me along. And he stops. And I look up
to his face and he is drenched and he moves his hands on
his chest, as if to wash himself with the sea, and he smiles
at me, a soft smile that tells me we have all the time in
the world, all the rest of our lives, and he tells me this so
I won't worry as he turns slowly around to look out to the
sea once more, before coming nearer.

And I find that I am moving toward him, faster, and I
am yanking my skirt up to my waist, and I leap up onto
his back. I throw my arms around his neck and I hook my
legs around his waist and he laughs a loud, sharp laugh of
surprise and his wrists come under my knees and lift at
me, hold me up, and I think that one day he will carry
our child on his back but for now I am glad it is me and he
carries me forward and I know what he is planning to do.

I laugh, and I cry, "Wait."

But he does not listen, he is going forward into the
water.

"Wait," I cry again but he can hear the thrill in my voice and he does not stop. Then I bend near, putting my mouth against his wet and salty ear. I say, "Don't you want me to be naked?" He stops. I am very conscious of those places where our flesh is touching. Beneath my leg, along my thigh, my forearms against his chest.

He turns and he wades toward the shore and I cling tight to him and for a moment I think I know what it feels like to have a father. I am small upon him and I am glad for that because the way he is big makes me safe and makes me loved and makes it so that I am not alone, and these are good things, but I am more glad for my thighs clutching his naked sides and more glad that my true father is nothing but smoke and air and I am more glad for where we are heading, out of the water now, and he does not stop, he is heading for the top of the beach and a stretch of low scrub grass there, before a dune. And beyond, the only light in the sky is spread along a jagged line of mountains and the light has turned red and we are in the dark shadow of the dune and he puts me down on the grass and my hands go to work instantly at my blouse, the buttons, the bow, it is off me and he is before me as I am doing this and watching my hands, watching what will be revealed beneath them. The blouse is gone and then my bra and he smiles at my nipples and the skirt is gone and my panties and then we are on the grass and my hand goes to this part of his body that at last I can see in my head and it is ardent now for me, unimpressed and withdrawn as it was with the sea, and if I am so much more exciting to his body than the South China Sea, I have no right to delay him, for I am rich with my own inner sea and I will drench and wash him now and I draw him into me right away, my Ben, my love, he will come into this place where our child has begun to grow.

How good it feels inside her, how good, there will be many more nights to go slow but on this shore on this night she wants me inside her quickly, she draws me there with her hand, and I move onto her and I look at the sea and the moon is out there, I didn't notice it before, though it's been there all along, hiding in its paleness, not show-ing itself, but now the daylight is almost gone and the moon has appeared, fat and golden.

I look at her face beneath me and her eyes are open and she is Tien, she is herself, I move in her and there's nothing here to fear at all. I am up Highway One in Viet-nam and this alien sea lies beside me and on my skin, and there is nothing of war, nothing of death, nothing of the past, there is only this joining of me and this woman, this Vietnamese woman, this woman I love, and I am at peace.

And then I rush and she digs hard at my back and her lips are against my ear and she cries out softly there, and only now are we related, only now, only this way, as we share one body, and then we slow and we stop and we lie still. Though I shift and am no longer inside her, this feeling between us does not change and she curls against me and I hold her, and for a long time, we lie still.

And the sky goes black and bursts with stars and the moon rises and grows small but it turns so white it almost hurts my eyes. I think she sleeps for a while. Then she wakes with a little start. I draw her closer and she whispers, "Yes."

"Did you have a dream?"

After a silence, she says, "In my sleep now I listen to my body."

"What does it say?"

She is quiet again, for a long while. Then she says, "What will we do tomorrow?"

"Make love."

She presses me onto my back and crawls directly on top of me, her chest hovering over my chest, her legs hugging my sides, her face eclipsing the moon. "That is a good answer," she says.

I can't see her eyes in the darkness, only the silhouette of her head. I lift my hand and with my fingertips I touch her lips and then trace up her check to her brow to the bridge of her nose, to her eye, feeling her eyelid close for me, I touch her there and her eye moves beneath my finger, the sign of dreaming.

I say, "Are you listening to your body right now?"

"Yes."

She didn't answer me the last time, so I move my hand from her face to her hip and I simply wait.

"I am glad I was born," she says.

"I am too."

"My father is dead."

"Yes."

The moon flares in my eyes. Her head has moved, she slides off me now, and I can see her face, I turn to her and I move to kiss her and I see her eyes shift to me and they are black, black as the empty spaces between the stars, and I close my own eyes with the touch of our lips. We kiss and she gently ends it and I look up into the sky and draw her close.

She says, "I almost was not born. I have always thought, now and then, that it made no difference, really. Now my body tells me that it is very important that I am alive."

I think of abortion. That her mother almost let Tien go. I want to tell her that I, too, am glad she is alive, but I sense something else running in her. I close my eyes against the brightness of the moon and I wait.

Then she says, "My mother made up a fairy tale for me once. She said it was about my father so I think there was a real story behind it. I loved a certain fairy tale of a dragon when I was a child, so she made it about dragons. In this story my father dies at the end. But it was really about *his* father, the part where I almost never was born."

I open my eyes. I turn my face out to the sky over the horizon, away from the moon. I feel a tiny stirring in me, like the flicker of one of the stars out there.

She says, "It happened that he almost died, my father's father. And if he had, then I never would have been born."

Something in me says to just keep quiet now But this flicker is actually a distant burning. I say, "What is the story? How did he almost die?"

"It is about a dragon—who turns out to be my grandfather —who goes every day into a fiery hole where he works . . . When I start saying this, it sounds silly. I do not know what parts are real and what parts are not."

"No," I say, and whatever is driving me to hear this is working on its own. I feel like I've floated off a ways down the beach. I'm out taking a smoke while this other part of me does some damn stupid thing. "It's not silly," I say. "What's the story she told?"

Tien adjusts her head into the dip between my shoulder and my chest. She says, "My grandfather's enemies try to kill him in this fiery hole. A place where he works. But he fights them and kills them instead. And it was after all this that my father is born. So you see, if he had died there instead, my father would not have been born and then he would not have gone to a distant land and met the princess—this was how my mother saw herself, I guess. But then I would not have been horn. And then . . ."

She stops abruptly, but there is already a stopping in me. The flicker is gone, the burning is gone, there is only cold now and a shift of gravity, a collapse in my chest. I try to wrench a thought from this place. The story is too familiar. Too familiar. The story my father told me about him going into the B-furnace stove in the Depression and the plant owner's goons trying to kill him. This was my story, and Tien's mother told her this thing just like it. Kim. Kim. But I can't remember ever telling Kim about my father and his fight in the mill. I try now. Try hard to remember. Nothing. This is good, I tell myself. They're different stories.

Tien finally finishes her thought. "And then I would not have made love to you. I would not be here tonight in my body, which I am very happy for."

I can say nothing. I think to ask for more details from her fairy tale. But it's about dragons and fiery holes and princesses—it is suddenly unimaginable that Kim could think of herself as a princess with me. Not even in a made-up story for her child. Never. This was a fairy tale and fairy tales are designed to make you think of your regular life. This fiery hole could be anything. But I am breathing heavily now, gasping for air. I gently untangle from Tien and I sit up.

"What is it?" she says.

I try to catch my breath. There is no reason for panic now. It was a fairy tale. But I realize we have to go on in the morning. We have to find Tien's mother.

"Ben?"

I finally say, "We have to find our clothes before the moon goes down."

My hand reaches, expecting his body, my eyes are still closed but I am climbing from the dark hole of sleep and there is just bed and pillow and the South China Sea is roaring and I sit up fast. The door to our room is standing open to the sea and there are breakers and the sun is shattered all over the water. My eyes hurt from the light. I shade them with my hand. "Ben?" I say and there is nothing. I begin to feel a panic in me. "Ben," I say louder, my feeling wound tight in the sound.

Then a shadow falls over my eyes. Ben is at the doorway. He steps in, moves to me. He is dressed. I look into his face, wait for my eyes to adjust. He stands over me and I can see him clearly now. His eyes arc soft, but something is wrong.

"What is it?" I say.

He takes my hand. "Nothing."

I rise up on my knees, quickly.

He says, "It's okay. There's nothing wrong."

I try to believe him. I realize it is about his eyes. I am naked here before him, but his eyes stay fixed on mine. I suddenly know what he will have us do. "You want to continue the search for her," I say. "Am I right?"

"Let's keep this room. Okay? We'll be back here by sunset."

"You are not my father."

"Of course not," he says, holding my hand tight. "I know that."

"I do not ask for a mother."

"Think of *me* as the child," he says. "I'm afraid of the thunder. I know it can't hurt me, but I hear it and I need to be reassured. That's what this is."

It occurs to me that this would be a time to tell him about what I am sure is going on inside my body. There should be no more talk of parents and children except for this real thing. And if I had awakened to find him sleeping beside me and he was naked and we were going no further on this trip, then I would. But I will not let our child be mixed up in this fear of his.

I say to him, "Let's do this as quickly as we can. I want to make love to you on this beach tonight."

He should say that this is what he wants, too. But he does not. He nods to me and he moves away, I suppose so he does not have to see me naked as I get up from the bed. I am angry. I feel my face glowing from this like I have been in the sun too long. His back is to me. He is at the door again. "Ben," I say to him.

He turns. I say, "Do you love me?"

"I'll show you how much tonight."

This is a good answer, I think. I am letting my anger go with this answer. He is very troubled. I can tell that. I do not know why this should have come on him again. It had to be out on the beach, after we made love. Perhaps he slept, too, and had a bad dream. I rise up from the bed and he is already turning his back to me once more.

He has the motor running in the car when I come from the villa's office. I get in and he asks, "Did she know where the village is?"

"Yes," I say. "I will tell you where to drive."

He nods and we pull away. I open my window and keep my face in the sea air. I must prepare myself now, to perhaps find my mother. The woman in the villa pulled out

a map to show me where the village is. She has two cous-
ins living there. It is called Trang Non, which means in
English "full moon." It is not a fishing village, as I thought.
They are woodcutters and coffee growers. In the mountains by the sea. My mother might not be there. She might
he dead. But if she is alive and we find her, I will say nothing. I will translate for Ben, if that is necessary, but only
what he needs in order to realize that this woman is a
stranger to him. Then we will go.

That is all the thought I wish to give to this day, and
we bump from the dirt road and turn onto Highway One,
and we travel on. I see only the turnings that we need
to make. We slide into Nha Trang along the main sea-
side boulevard, lined with coconut palms, and then we
go over two bridges and we arc through the city and we
pass a great white statue of the Buddha looking out to sea,
desiring nothing, except to sit by the sea and be perfect,
and we take the cutoff that goes along the Hon Chong
beaches.

There are mountains near us, but I do not look. One of
these mountains is supposed to look like a reclining princess who married a giant who saw her bathing naked and
made a handprint on some big rock and then she died. Or
something like that. I am not caring to think of fairy tales
at the moment. Things are suddenly very much what they

seem to be. We are driving among mountains and rocks. That is all.

And then I have to find a gravel side road and we slow and I find the place and we start to climb for a ways and then the road cuts back toward the sea and we are shrouded in trees and the road squeezes into one lane and bounces us around a turn and there is only a grassy field in front of us and a wall of trees. We stop. Ben looks at me.

"We have to walk from here," I say.

He turns off the engine and sets the emergency brake and we sit quietly for a moment. Finally he says, "I'm sorry."

"I know."

And then I find myself saying, "How sorry?"

He looks at me, a little surprised.

I am, too, at the thrashing that has begun inside me.

"What do you mean?" he says.

I say, "Are you sorry enough to turn around now and take me away from here and never think about all this again?"

"We've come this far."

"I am afraid. If she is here. I am afraid of her."

"There's nothing to be afraid of."

He is right. I cry out to myself that he is right. If she is here, then she left me for herself, just for herself. Some part of me is afraid of that. But that is an old hurt. A thing long dead, it means nothing to me now. This is nothing to fear. But the thrashing goes on. From a darker wind. But if there is some other fear, then we must go on, or that fear will never end.

So I take Ben's face in my two hands and I draw him to me and I kiss him on the mouth, not caring if he is ready to do this in return, though he does kiss me, but not enough, really, not as much as I am kissing him, but I do not care. My mother will not come between us. She will not hurt us. I will take these two hands and strangle her to death if we find her and she tries to hurt Ben and me. But she will be a stranger to him, and to me, as well, and we will be back in this car soon.

"I am all right now," I say. "I want to do this thing and be done with it."

"I do too," he says. I expect him to get out at once. But he does not. He turns my face now, with his fingertips just under my chin, and he kisses me on the lips. Very light. Very brief. But he does kiss me.

I lean against the car door and I feel as if I have no strength. I do not need a mother. I press hard. It is for Ben. And the door opens and I move and I find myself out in the middle of the grassy place. The grass runs on to what looks like a cliff edge, and beyond is a slice of the sea. We have climbed a long way up already. Against the jade of the water is a distant fishing boat with a sail curved like a Chinese sword.

Now we can also see a wide path cut in the tree line and we move toward it. My legs are heavy. Ben does not take my hand. And we are into the trees and climbing some more, sea pines for a while, swaying high above us, silent, my legs are aching from the slope of this path, and I am breathing heavily and I can hear Ben breathing heavily and these are two breaths now, it strikes me, very hard, two separate breaths on this path, not the one breath we made last night, and I touch the baby, and I climb. And finally the pines thin and the path levels and we come out into bright sun and another clearing. To our left is a gentle slope and coffee trees planted in rows, and before us, straight on, shrouded in bamboo thickets and willows, is the village. A dog barks up ahead, out of sight, and another.

"Be careful of the dogs," I say to Ben. "Village dogs can be vicious."

She warns me about the dogs and wherever it is in my head that I've been hiding since last night, I'm chased out now. This is how we began, and she should be pissed as hell at me or scared as hell but here she is warning me about the dogs again and the only thing in her voice is concern for me. Ahead is the place. There's bamboo all around and some trees, but I can see the palm leaf roofs of the houses and a track of smoke rising and I can smell a wood fire and the dogs are barking like crazy. I should say to her, You're right about the goddamn dogs, let's get the hell out of here. I turn to her and she's gone. For a moment, I think she's heading back down the path and this is good. Let her run like hell. I'll follow her. She can just whisper *Fuck no* and we can go away and if I have to live with some weird goddamn fears once in a while, I can do it. There's just no way ever to know for sure. Except if we end up in the States, which I figure we have to, there's blood types and there's DNA or whatever, so there is a way and I'll have to know sooner or later and someday she's going to want to know, too. Like as soon as she starts thinking about children of our own.

But she hasn't bolted. She's moving off to the right, toward the sea. I follow. She's moving slow and dreamy and the sea is beautiful out there, it's clean and the line of the horizon is sharp and wide, simple, things are simple there, and though I can't hide the fear now, it's too close—just along the path and behind some bamboo—I want this clean sword-cut of an answer, and I know it'll be clean and it'll be okay, some part of me is saying that louder and louder, to hell with fairy tales, and Tien moves to the cliff edge and stops.

I come up behind her and put my hands on her shoulders. Her hands come up and touch mine. I kiss her hair and then I look beyond her and over the edge of the cliff, and it's sheer, falling far, far away down to the rocks and the sea.

We stand like that for a long while. The breeze rustles at us but things feel very calm, all of a sudden. We made love last night along this sea. It's ours. Her hands are on mine. I look down at them, and I see the moons there and the grinding starts again inside me.

"It's time," I say.

She nods and turns and she moves off without another word or another touch, and I feel this withholding—suddenly all that I feel about her hands is the yearning to take them in mine, to kiss those pale moons—but I follow her, across the grass and onto a wide dirt path, and the trees take up on each side and then the bamboo comes in and the path narrows and we turn once and again, surrounded by the stalks of bamboo sectioned like bone, and suddenly we are before a little square with a great stone cistern in the middle and ringed by little houses of thatch and palm. A woman is dipping a ladle into the water in the cistern. Her face is hidden by a conical straw hat. A dog barks nearby. I look and he is peeking around a house and when I meet his eyes he disappears. The woman turns her head. She is very old.

Tien crosses to her and the old woman greets her and they speak for a moment. First Tien and then the woman and then Tien again and the woman nods her head and it is a clear yes she is saying and she motions beyond the cistern, off down another path, and I try to keep still but I can't, not for a moment, I come forward and Tien is turning to me and her face is drawn tight.

"She's here," I say.

"There's someone here with my mother's name," she says.

"Where?"

Tien says another few words in Vietnamese to the woman who is smiling broadly at me and nodding her head over and over and Tien moves off and I follow and it's hard just to walk, just to put one foot in front of the other in a regular way, but we do walk, slower than before if anything. Tien is having trouble moving.

"It's okay," I say to her. "I'm with you. This won't take long."

She smiles up at me. My words sound confident. Maybe I am. Maybe I am or I wouldn't be wanting to bolt down this path to wherever it is we're going. She touches my hand, briefly, and my penis instantly stirs. But this first. This first.

And we are moving through another maze of growth, and chickens scatter before us, clucking furiously, plunging into a tiny break in the bamboo, and we come out of the maze and Tien stops.

There are two small thatched houses before us. She turns to the one on the left and two women are crouching flat-footed in front, their knees up by their faces, two sexless middle-aged women, dark from the sun, their hair put up in buns, straw hats beside them. And between them is a small package, cut open, of lime paste and a scattering of rust-colored arcea nuts and the pale green betel leaves, and one of the women, the nearest one, has just rolled a hit of this stuff to chew. Two aging women getting high on a Saturday morning. And the nearest one puts the roll in her mouth and she looks up at us and I am looking only at her mouth, and her teeth and gums are red from this stuff already, and then I look at her eyes and they are glazed a little and they look into mine and I don't know how it is that I know but I do, because I never carried her face with me, except her eyes, and her eyes always seemed memorable from being like all the other eyes in this country, but now they're before me and they're Kim's, the woman is Kim, and I'm taking all this in slow, and I hear Tien's voice start up in Vietnamese and it is very distant and Kim's eyes swing away from me. There is a moment now. Tien's voice fades in my head but Tien remains, the smell of her and the press of her body remain, and I realize that I am complete. But I am complete only with her body and through her body, hers, my child's, the body of my child, and Kim's face is on her daughter and it stays and stays and there is no sound in the world and I am poised in some high place and will fall, but in this moment of suspension I am whole, at last, whole, and now in this moment a sound breaks in me, the South China Sea, and in this moment the dark beneath me is the dark of the shore beneath a golden moon, and Tien's body is imprinted on mine, and in this act of our love, her heart and her mind and her voice are there too, and she is in my blood, and I am in her, in all ways in her, and from this moment, I feel the lift of my penis for her, and now it is a gesture that will tear us apart, my child and me, because it is for her that my body is doing this, for my child, and a terrible heat begins in that lift, in that place of my sex, a deep, hot roiling that spreads fast from my groin to my legs to my hands to my head and Kim's face is on mine now and her eyes have gone wide and I look at my daughter, my lover, and my body yearns for hers, yearns even as this thing spreads through me like the fire that I wish had taken my father, taken him in that fiery hole and killed the seed of me that lies now inside my own child, my own.

Ben and I come out of the path and the house has two figures before it and my heart is beating so hard I can feel it in my throat and these figures are both women and they are coarse women, low-class women, drugging themselves with arcea and betel, and the house is ragged and of the worst construction, unplaned sticks and bamboo tied with palm cord, and I am not even looking at the faces of these women. There is a sour rushing in me, like the fumy wind of motorcycles in the city, and I want this over now. I say in my native language, "I am looking for Le Thi Huong."

The face nearest me turns and the rushing stops. I go very still inside. Her eyes rise to me and they are blank. She does not recognize me. I was only a child when she last saw me. But I know this face. She is not dead. She has been crouching here all along, chewing and forgetting, and she saved her own life from a threat that never was, and after that, she wanted nothing from the past, including her daughter. And I have nothing to ask her now.

Nothing to say. There is only one thing more and I do not even need her for this. Ben already knows she is a stranger to him. But I hear my voice shaping the words anyway. I say, "Do you know this man?" and I already know the answer and I will hear it and Ben and I will walk away and I will never tell her who I am.

I follow the movement of her face, the lift of her eyes, back to Ben, and I look at him and his eyes are wild, though they are fixed, fixed hard, not moving, but I feel the wildness behind them, and I look at my mother and her own eyes widen, as if she has looked into the morning sky and a great ragged body had suddenly appeared, blocking the sun, ready to fall with teeth and claws flashing, and they flash now in me, the shape falls into me and begins to slash away, and I turn to Ben one last time, desperate to see a flush of relief there, a laugh, but he turns his wild eyes on me, and they are so beautiful, these eyes, these dark eyes, all the gentleness I have ever dreamed of is here in these eyes, and my hands ache to plunge to that sweet hard center of him and draw his body into mine, at this moment, at this very moment, I want to cling to my father's secret body, and I cry out, I hear myself cry a wordless thing and I know that whatever horror is in this sound, there is also my woman's love for him, I ache as a lover for my father, and I break away and I move into the bamboo shade and I turn in the path and I am running

now and my foot falls and falls and each fall strokes that
secret part of my body and he is in my head and we are
by the sea and it is night and he falls in me and falls and
strokes and I burst from the path and across the little
square and past the cistern and I know where I am going
now and I pulse in my sex and I pulse there and I cry out
again at this terrible thing and there is nothing to stop it
but this thing I must do and I am in the path again leading
from the village and then I am in the open field.

I slow, I slow, I quake in my sex and I am nearly blind
from the sun here and I push my body on, I push on, and
the South China Sea waits and my eyes clear and the sea
is enormous and it is green darkness like the dark inside
the banyan tree and I move and I think of my child and
the quaking makes it hard to put one foot before the
other now and this is the child of my father inside me,
and this much the quaking knows, this much is clear in
the secret path I follow now across this field: we cannot all of us remain here in this life together, we cannot
remain.

And I move more quickly and the sea grows larger and
the edge is near and the wind beats at me but I am stronger I will go now and the clean cut of the cliff edge will be
mine, another step another and a hard thing suddenly cir-
cles me, an arm is around my waist and jerks me back and
Ben's voice is in my ear. "Tien." And the arm loosens and

I turn and his face is above me filling the sky and his eyes are deep and I could leap there, I think, I could drown there and he pulls back from me, only a little bit, only for a moment, and we are touching eyes we are touching still and I say the word I do not mean to say, I do not want to say, I say "Father," and we try to hold on to that word, I feel him straining like me trying to hold that word between us and the ache is wild in me and I feel it in him and then we are in each other's arms and our mouths are touching from that ache and from what I know is goodbye and I am ready to go but he says, "Only one of us, my darling," and his arms slip away and he is a blur now I cannot move he turns and he steps and he leaps and he flies he flies and he is gone.

Father, I am here. I left the dark burning of this incense for you. I offer your spirit the peace that comes from the love and prayers and devotion of your daughter and I ask you for the harmony and the peace that a father can give to his family.

I wait. I do not blame you for this pain. It is the suffering that comes from desire, my love. I desire the lie of our two nights of

touching. The true lie of it. I desire, as well, that moment cling-
ing to your back. I would find peace in just that. I light another
stick of incense now, and another. I would fill my lungs with the
smoke of your soul. I ask for you to give me peace, even as I offer
you the same thing. We will try each night. We will try.

My father, my love, on this day, one month after her birth, I
took our daughter to a pagoda, and a monk poured special water
from the altar into a white jasmine flower. Then I held her before
a great sandalwood statue of Long Vuong, the Dragon King, and
our daughter's dark eyes were open and she was very still and the
monk put the blossom in my hand and I brought it gently over
her face. My hand was very steady, Father, and she waited with
great patience, a patience that I pray I will learn from her. And
I tipped the blossom ever so slowly, and the water swelled and
swelled, and then a single drop formed at the sharp tip of a petal,
and as if she knew what gift this was, our daughter opened her
mouth and the drop fell onto her tongue.

Father, her words will be sweet as jasmine all her life. One day
her sweet words will join mine and rise with this smoke to you.
She will atone for us, my darling. She will love you, always, with
the pure love of a child who owes her life to her father. And I will
love you, too, as I have been given to do, always.